A MIRACLE OF WAR

Robert J. M. Horn and C. David Brown

DORRANCE
PUBLISHING CO
EST. 1920
PITTSBURGH, PENNSYLVANIA 15238

Dorrance Publishing Co
585 Alpha Drive
Pittsburgh, PA 15238
Visit our website at *www.dorrancebookstore.com*

ISBN: 979-8-88729-147-5
eISBN: 979-8-88729-647-0

THIS BOOK IS IN MEMORY OF

C. DAVID BROWN

1953 to 2013

ACKNOWLEDGEMENTS

TO THE EDITORS
JENNIFER BOAZ.
AND
NANCY JANIKE
AND

THOSE WHOSE SUPPORT AND ENCOURAGEMENT MADE THE COMPLETION OF THIS BOOK THE MIRACLE OF WAR POSSIBLE.

SHIRLEY HORN
THE PETILLON FAMILY

Foreword

This is a story of the past, although a not too distant one. If you read this laden with the modern prejudice that folks in the 1800s were less intelligent, more insensitive, rigid, intolerant, overly sentimental, too religious, too unquestioning of their world, et al., then you are not a good candidate to understand the forces that shape history. Indeed this era forged the foundation upon which your modern America would exist.

The task of a proper war historian is to accurately march you from point A to point B with copious facts and footnotes and quotes. For those of us that have studied the Civil War, or War Between the States, or the War of Northern Aggression, no era has produced more books. A few are great, many are very good, more are average but readable and entertaining, and large quantities are best left unread. No era of American history has had a greater impact on our people or spawned as many volumes.

The purpose of a historical fiction writer is to blend the information of the historian with that of a storyteller. It is our quest in this novel to explain the why of the key players of the last eighteen months of the war on the Confederate side. We do this through thoughts, projected dialogue, and actions based on historical fact gleaned from the hard facts and known details. Often actual conversations and character traits are paraphrased from actual recounting by the participants or witnesses or in reports and diaries and the like.

The time of battles, events, places, key individuals, period language, and customs are accurate.

The authors do indulge in a bit of history buff fantasy at the conclusion of each battle phase. General R.E. Lee appears with a brief and concise analysis of what happened and who was the better general with the better plan. We strive to humanize the great Lee without removing an iota of dignity to the greatest of American generals before or after. If that is too much fantasy for you, then skip those sections. We suspect that all of you legions of Civil War history buffs out there will not.

Robert J. M. Horn and C. David Brown

Contents

IT IS AN ARMY OF FAITH

It is an army of faith. With few exceptions, its soldiers believe in God. Most are Protestants, but there are many Catholics and some Jews as well. By their words and deeds, diaries, journals, letters, and remembrances, they live a much more verbally expressed communion with their Lord than we would be accustomed to in 2019. Their regiments and many of the individual companies had a chaplain.

It starts as a grand picnic adventure. Most are certain it will be over in a few weeks or months at the worst, right after they whip the "Damn Yankees." None can foresee that this most horrid of American Wars will last four years, cost at least 620,000 lives out of a total pre-war population of 3.1 million, and cripple the South economically for a century.

As they march on towards their exciting adventure, most have never been further than twenty miles from home. They have no inkling that one in three of them will die before the war's end, almost all will be wounded at least once, and that the South will lose the flower of the male gender for a generation.

They are a product of their time and environment as we all are. They would be bemused, bewildered, and appalled at the politically correct mythology of our time. They fight to protect their homes, families, and states, and few could ever aspire to own a slave, much less in multiples.

They do not hate blacks. The refuse of the carpetbaggers and scalawags of the post-war reconstruction era will spawn the Jim Crow laws, a legacy that haunts the South to this day. Most of them have a vague notion that their leaders have tried to figure out a way to end slavery, but nobody knows quite how to do it.

It is a simpler society. And with that is no governmental safety net. There are no government social services, Welfare, Social Security, Medicare, Workmen's Compensation, or regulatory agencies. The Federal government is tiny and very weak. These men and their families rely on their relatives, neighbors, and friends to assist when times grow difficult for them.

They do not call themselves Americans nor do their Federal foes. Keep in mind these men are provincial and are most loyal to their communities and states. So they go off to serve as Texans, Georgians, Virginians, and so on. It will not be until after the war that the antagonists and protagonists refer to themselves as Americans.

You cannot study history and do it justice through the prism of your time, in this case 2020. We are a product of our time just as they were of theirs. Do not fall in the great trap of being judgmental. They were just as intelligent as you and had the same motivations, hopes, dreams, and aspirations. They love their families and especially their sweethearts (the term girlfriend did not exist) and wives. The letters that they write home (I have read hundreds) are touching and poignant. Many are surprisingly heartfelt to wives on matters of intimacy. I won't go further, but you get the idea. So are the letters from the wives. Mail was not censored back then but unusually late in arriving. It is certainly clear that the soldiers loved their sweethearts or wives and had them on their minds continuously. They are a very sentimental group of men.

They love songs of love and have many favorites. Lorena, When This Cruel War is Over, The Yellow Rose of Texas, and many others and sing them around their campfires. Most units are blessed with a fiddle or banjo player. Of course they have their favorite marshalling songs of which The Bonnie Blue Flag and Dixie are the most popular. And they also love hymns of the sentimental religious type, like Amazing Grace.

A surprising number were literate or semi-so. The semi-literate could read better than they could write. This led to a lot of phonetic spelling. English was just as baffling to sort out in sentence structure and spelling just as it is today. There were no public-school systems then. There were a strong number of little private schools. The teachers were all male and practiced their avocation on a subsistence of bartered trade goods and small donations. Many of these men would make efficient sergeants and junior officers in the Great War.

They are and will always be outnumbered and they knew it. But they had many intangibles going for them. Generally they are much better led. Then as today, a disproportionate percentage of the pre-war Federal Army hails from the South. Not only does the South have a large cadre of West Pointers, including most of the best officers in the Federal Army, it also has a large contingent of graduates from Southern military academies, like V.M.I., the Citadel, what will become L.S.U., and many others. Militia units (predecessors to what we would call the National Guard) are large and very popular in the pre-war South.

And since most of the men were farmers, they were experienced out-doorsmen and possessed excellent marksmanship skills. In this respect, they had an edge over their Federal opponents, especially those from the big cities and the northeast.

By the end of 1862, the cowards and shirkers are all gone. The remaining men have coalesced into a unique group that is much more the sum of the whole than the individual parts. From the crucible of trial by fire, they will forge a special "espirit de corps" (Southerners would pronounce that "as spree day core"). Not an aura of arrogance but rather one of quiet confidence and pride. They will take a rather reverse satisfaction in being able to endure a host of privations, including almost constant hunger, poor diet, meager pay, and rarely payment thereof, ragged clothing and shoe gear, abysmal medical care, and being constantly outnumbered. Through the course of un-ending adversity, they will endure and prevail against a much mightier and better equipped foe. This sense of hardiness will lead to a distinct and very evident sense of identity whether they are called as a group Confederates, Secesh (for Secessionists), Rebels, Johnnie Rebs, or just Rebs.

They will also express themselves in something totally unique to them, the famous "Rebel Yell." So the goose bump raising, spine tingling, nerve rattling, and downright eerie, the high-pitched wail becomes a Confederate weapon. No linguist seems to be able to explain how it developed or its origins. The best answer I can provide is that it emanates from the multitude of Southern accents that range from New Mexico to Oklahoma, through the thirteen official Southern states in the C.S.A., and on to Maryland. In any case, it sprang up simultaneously across thousands of miles and was a verbal group manifestation of identity.

They respect their opponents and treat them kindly when captured if they fight by the rules of decency. As the War drags on and the Federal policy shifts more to an expansion of warfare on the civilian populace, God help the Federals caught molesting women, children, or old folks, looting homes or persons, burning civilian personal property, destroying crops and live-stock, or razing homesteads. The perpetrator (s) usually received the quick impersonal justice of a Colt revolver. And this happened thousands of times in the last two years of war.

Prior to the start of this journey, let's demolish some myths with cold hard facts.

Myth: The big battles, like Gettysburg, Vicksburg, Shiloh, Atlanta, Antietam, and Chancellorsville, were where most of the causalities occurred. There were hundreds of mid-size battles and thousands of skirmishes that in total caused as many or more losses over the course of the war.

Myth: Hollywood and many high school textbooks would have you believe that the average Rebel soldier was usually pitifully reduced to throwing rocks and dirt clods, short of ammunition and possessing a handful of old flintlock muskets and squirrel shotguns. Actually the C.S.A. imported several hundred thousand of the top of the line British Enfield rifles. These weapons were comparable to the U.S. Springfield rifles, except they were two pounds lighter and better suited to the faster moving Rebel infantry. An average soldier could kill at 200 to 300 yards or more. The C.S.A. also imported large quantities of British Whitworth sharpshooter rifles with telescopic sights that had a range of two miles or more. The Confederates also imported some British Whitworth revolutionary breech loading rifled cannons with unmatched range and accuracy.

In addition the C.S.A. produced large quantities of copied model 1860 Springfield rifles thanks to the genius of Ordnance Bureau Chief Brigadier

General Gorgas. Gorgas also produced large quantities of artillery identical to the Federal cannon in use.

Thanks to the chemistry genius of Colonel Rains, the Rebel forces were never short of powder or shot. Even though ingredients were in short supply.

Next myth: It was an all-white army. No, sir. Soldiers of Mexican/Spanish descent in Texas and New Mexico fought as Confederates in the Southwest. The Indians in the Indian Territory (present day Oklahoma) largely sided with the South. Comprised largely of the Five Civilized Tribes dispossessed of their land by the Federal government and forcibly removed, they had little love of the Federals. Their leader, Cherokee and C.S.A. Brigadier General Stand Waite, would be the last general officer to surrender to Union forces. There were several hundred thousand free blacks in the South, and many of them served. The transportation and engineer units of the Rebel forces were largely armed blacks, and they fought as Federal cavalry raiders admitted in their after-action reports. Also, almost without exception, many of the slave owners that did bring a body servant with them freed them, and they fought alongside their former master. There were also thousands of mulattos or mixed bloods, especially in the Louisiana regiments. After the war, the veterans formed an organization called the United Confederate Veterans that in turn spawned today's Sons of Confederate Veterans. Thousands of blacks were members. There is a roadside park between College Station and Hempstead, Texas that has a marker to one that was an esteemed member of the local community. There are many more.

Their clothing did present a bedraggled appearance. Often his shirt was cotton made by his mother, sister, or sweetheart. His pants were usually much mended. Many wore Federal pants gleaned from previous battlefields. Their jacket or coat was usually faded gray, or more commonly as the war progressed, butternut in color and made of wool. All clothing edges tended to be frayed. His shoes were anything he could find, and normally the Federal dead were the chief source of supply. Many men went barefoot or wore tattered footwear in the last part of the war. Most wore a slouch hat, sometimes pinned up on one side of the brim if he felt stylish. Some wore the French kepi style cap as did most of the Federals. Most of the men wore their hair long and were as presentable as the camp barber could make them. Viewed as a group, they were a motley bunch, if you judge simply by appearance. Oddly this polyglot of non-uniformity created an impish sense of pride and identity. As a staff officer of Federal General Meade viewed them, "A more sinewy, tawny, formidable-looking set of men could not be...they handle their weapons with terrible effect. Their great characteristic is their stoical manliness; they...look you straight in the face, with as little animosity as if they had never heard a gun."

In their gear and how they wore it, they looked very much like their Federal counterparts. Across his body, he slung a blanket roll in an oil cloth, the latter another item gleaned from the Federal dead. In the opposite direction, he ran his haversack. In this he carried his comb and razor, toothbrush, a piece of soap, a pencil, a washcloth, a small mirror, sometimes a needle case, and sometimes his tobacco and pipe. Often letters from home, especially from a wife or sweetheart, were housed there and a daguerreotype (picture) and [or locket of a wife's or sweetheart's hair]. Many carried a compact bible or a New Testament. If he had any, his cooked rations went in there, too, along with any food he might forage, such as plums, berries, potatoes, wild greens, and such. Outside his haversack, he carried his tin cup, a multi-purpose tool. A few carried saucepans, but most of the pots and skillets were in the regimental wagons. Opposite his haversack, he might sling his tin canteen or sometimes around his neck hanging in the middle of his back. Sometimes he wore a leather cartridge case of either C.S.A. or Federal issue. More commonly he carried his cartridges in his pockets. His all-purpose utility tool was his bayonet. It was used for roasting meat, as a candleholder when inverted and stuck in the ground, sticking stray pigs or chickens, and as an entrenching tool.

His diet and the way he prepared his meager food was nothing to write home about to the womenfolk. The Confederate government was acutely aware of the debilitating effects of scurvy that can be prevented by adequate quantities of vegetables. However, the Southern supply system delivered these on an all too irregular basis. Vitamins did not exist in either word or form. The most common mainstay was salt pork cut in thick slices, somewhat like today's Canadian bacon and cornmeal. From this they concocted a dish called "cush" or "cush-cush" or "whoosh." It consisted of bacon grease, cornmeal mixed with water, and bits of bacon. If they had a skillet or a saucepan, they would bake the mix into a greasy cornbread or dip a stick or rifle ramrod into the goop and fry over their campfire.

Why did they fight with such tenacity to retain possession of their battle flags? Seems quirky by today's standards, doesn't it? The flags represented their local communities. The South had no flag-making companies. The ladies in the locale of a particular regiment gathered in a giant sewing bee and made the flags by hand, stitch by stitch. I've viewed many in museums across the South, and you can see the difference in the work. Often little touches particular to a community would be added as a garnish. No two flags were quite alike, and there was a story behind each. As the war progressed, many units sewed on the names of the battles they had fought in. Most of the flags that survive today are bullet riddled and blood stained. And many of the flags were identifiable to the unit and its locale. The Texas regiments also carried the Lone Star Flag, General Cleburne's Division in the Army of the Tennessee carried a blue flag with the St. Andrews Cross, and many units carried the bonnie blue flag design or their own state insignia.

As the war went on and on, desertion was a major problem on both sides. But there is more to it than the surface would imply. If a Federal soldier went home, he was likely tired of the fighting and the gore and the uneasy sense that he was an uninvited invader. When Rebs went home, it more often was due to heartrending plea letters from their womenfolk speaking of looming starvation, family illness, and Yankee depredations. A rather tacit and widespread system evolved where men would slip off when not much was happening. They would put in crops for themselves, and neighbors, pick up what supplies they could, like cloth, sewing gear, and the like, plus letters and come back. In this war, the soldier's main man was his regimental commander. On his return, the colonel would go through the motions of chewing him out with a mock straight face and give him a few extra chores. Everybody would wink and grin and that was that.

I can give you some personal examples. My great-great-grandfather (author David Brown's), Samuel Miller, fought in the ghastly battles of Iuka and Corinth in 1862 in northern Mississippi. Come winter he slipped away to his nearby home. I'm glad he did for Sam's wife became pregnant, which is why I exist to write this. Six months later, after surviving the siege of Vicksburg in which his 38th Mississippi Regiment saw hand to hand combat, Sam was the last documented soldier killed in the siege.

Another great-great-grandfather, Rancey Myers, rode with Nathan Bedford Forrest's cavalry and also deserted briefly and returned. Rancey was wounded in the groin horizontally (a gut shot was sure death) when his regiment drove off a Federal raiding party of larger size in an old-fashioned cavalry charge, foiling an attempt to burn a key high trestle bridge of the Mississippi Central railroad. He returned to fight and fathered children after the war. Another close call for me!

Men who had key skills, like shoemakers, tailors, coopers, and blacksmiths, also frequently went home in search of supplies and returned. I think my own great-grandfather, Alexander Brown, a blacksmith, may fit in this group. He deserted also because he had an ailing wife, and it was in a winter period when little was happening in the defense of Mobile. The regimental roll records of the last part of the war are largely missing for his 13th C.S.A. Cavalry Regiment, so he may have returned in time for the Battle of Mobile at the war's end. Or maybe he didn't. His regiment's camp was a short distance away, so if they wanted him, they knew where to find him.

With typical Southern informality, it was that kind of war.

As the war went on, the men became pretty good tacticians. They could size up a piece of ground and form an accurate opinion if they could hold it or take it. If they were well led by an officer they respected that commanded with bravery and intelligence, they would try to do the impossible if he asked it of them. It was a given that they expected their Colonels, Brigade, and Division Commanders to lead them from the front. This led to well-motivated troops, but by the war's twilight, the Confederate officer corps was largely decimated.

So again why did they fight under such underdog odds? To paraphrase what many a captured Rebel soldier said when queried by his Federal captors, "This is our land, and you're on it."

It had not been that long ago that Virginian Thomas Jefferson wrote the Declaration of Independence. Jefferson wrote:

We hold these truths to be self-evident. That all men are created equal, that they are endowed by their Creator with certain unalienable Rights, that among these are Life, Liberty, and the pursuit of Happiness. That to secure these rights, Governments are instituted among Men, deriving their just powers from the consent of the governed. That whenever any Form of Government becomes destructive to these ends, it is the Right of the People to alter or abolish it, and to institute a new Government, laying its foundation on such principles and organizing its powers in such form, as to them shall seem most likely to affect their Safety and Happiness.

None could foresee, not even the very wise, what the terrible saga of 1861 to 1865 would bring.

"TRAVELLER" A RELATIONSHIP BEGINS

On a hot summer day in Virginia, I was sent to the auction for possible sale. This was a special auction and was held for horses of excellent breeding, young strong mounts that would serve their owner well for years to come. The talk in the stables was all about who would end up where and with what kind of a master. Visions of grandeur were running amuck, and I rather took all this in stride realizing that my purchaser was way beyond my control.

Tomorrow we will all be led to a viewing area, and the buyers will look at our leg strength, our teeth, and our eyes. The auctioneer will start the bidding, and the day's festivities will include food and beverage for all. The men will tell stories about the great horses they have had in the past, and the truth shall be forgotten in the flow of storytelling.

It is morning now, and the grooms are coming to take us to the viewing area and the riding track. From there we will go to the auction area for the bidding to start. The weather is good, and there is a large crowd gathered to my right, and they seem to be very jovial and excited as we pass by them.

It is time for the viewing, and many men are looking me over. It seems like a hundred have touched me, and I must admit I am enjoying all the attention. There is a tall man with deep brown eyes whose touch is very gentle, and he continues to stare at me as others come by to examine me.

I am being led to the riding track; it is oval-shaped and lined with huge live oak trees, and the ground is very soft and level. Only those who have given their word that they are bidding on a particular horse are allowed to ride. The same rider has ridden several horses, and some of my fellow horses have shown little enthusiasm for this exercise. Soon it will be my turn, and I hope that my behavior and performance will warrant a good owner.

There are about fifteen men who have ridden me and one to go, and it's the tall man with the dark brown eyes. He looks like an aristocrat and maybe a little unknowable because he has been very serious and has not been mixing with the others. The auctioneer has called him Robert and said that he thought he would like my performance. It is time for me to show off a little, so I have raised my head high and watched my bridle shake for Robert.

Robert is now being called Mr. Lee from Virginia and has run his gentle hand along my neck and is up on my back like I was made for him. His hand is firm on my reins, and I know this man is a horseman of some quality. With each command he gives me, I respond quickly and in a fluid manner to his delight. The bidding has begun, and I don't pretend to understand what the auctioneer is saying, but I can see the hands being raised, and one of them is that of Mr. Robert E. Lee. The price is getting higher and higher, and Mr. Lee's wife is looking at him like she is suffering from some sort of malady as he continues to bid. It's over, and the winning bid is a small fortune, and I now belong to Colonel Robert E. Lee! The gentlemen with him are congratulating him on his purchase of me, and one of them they call "Old Pete" wants to know what my name shall be. Without hesitation Robert has said I am to be called "Traveller." Little did we both know that I would carry him thousands of miles in a great civil war that would define this nation for decades to come

A TIME OF CONCERN

My days are peaceful and spent in a beautiful place called Arlington, the mansion home of Robert E. Lee and his family. With every passing day, there are more riders coming to our home with messages for Mr. Lee. The horses they ride talk to me about an unrest that is coming over the land and about a man called John Brown and his soldiers who are shooting up an area of the Midwest. There is sadness in Robert's eyes, and when we ride with others, like the man they call "Fuss and Feathers," he talks about not dissolving the Union. The Union must be preserved, or it will be disastrous to the nation as a whole. There are misunderstandings between states, and some feel their rights are in danger of disappearing.

An election is coming soon, and there is a gala event scheduled for this evening at the White House, and my master and I are going to attend. Many of the men he fought alongside of in the Mexican War will be there, including General Scott, the Commander, and Chief of the Military. It was he who said my master was the best combat officer he had ever seen, and their admiration for each other was well-known to all. Sam Grant, Twigs, Longstreet, Sherman, Sheridan, Stuart, they were all there for the festivities. Outside this magnificent building, I stood next to several military mounts that all seemed to know what those inside did not know or would not admit to–that this nation was going to be torn apart very soon.

A rider is approaching, and his horse is lathered and worn out. The rider's expression has danger all over it, and he is dusty and has been in the saddle at a high speed for many hours. The honor guards at the door have stopped him and are questioning him. His horse told me that John Brown is at Harpers Ferry and has taken the arsenal there by force. Now there is much commotion by the French doors as Colonel Lee has been ordered to take troops and reclaim Harpers Ferry. Many of the junior officers are asking him if they can come along; there is a strong sense of admiration of my partner.

So much for John Brown and Harpers Ferry–he never knew what the hell hit him. It was faster than I could say "More hay, please." The soldiers are very happy, and some are coming by and just touching me as if to say "Well done." Someone else, through debts, slavery, crimes, or some other reason, owns four out of every seven Americans. It is truly a time for concern.

A MAN FROM ILLINOIS

Some time has passed, and it is May of 1860, and my partner Colonel Lee has invited many guests to a fine picnic at his home in Arlington overlooking the Capital. Washington is blooming with cherry blossoms, and all manner of life is emerging from a hard winter. I can smell southern fried chicken cooking in the summer kitchen, and the servants are preparing long tables for the guests.

There are more horses here than I have seen in my entire life and many pulling carriages that are inlaid with silver and fine leather. The politicians and the military personnel with their wives seem to dominate the guest list. The last of the guests are arriving, and even though there is strife across the land, this day there shall be calmness for all to remember. Here comes one of my favorite people, Lo Armistead, a fine man with a somewhat twisted sense of humor. He is at it again, waving a buttered ear of hot corn on the cob in front of my nose and at the same time wanting to know if I have been chasing any mares around the pasture.

As the day has worn on, they have decided to put most of the horses in the corral with me, and that suits me. There is one I really want to horse around with and talk to because he led the carriage of a tall, gaunt man from Illinois who is running for President of the country. He says his partner's name is Mr. Lincoln and that he is six-foot-four inches tall and he is a great storyteller. Mr. Lincoln, it seems, has a great abiding love for the Union and does not wish to see it dissolved. He came here today to talk to mostly Southerners about preserving the Union and where the direction of the nation must be headed if it is to survive. He believes in God and His will, yet has no religious affiliation with any group. Mr. Lincoln says that government should be of laws rather than of men.

Oh, this will be interesting! Here are Colonel Lee and Mr. Lincoln to see me. Nothing like a good rubbing hand to make my day, and Mr. Lincoln seems to be a gentleman just like Colonel Lee. They both seem to be excellent judges of horses of course, but more than that, they seem to enjoy each other's company as they share their views on the critical issues of state's rights and the economics of both North and South. Both men agree that if Mr. Lincoln is elected this fall, there will be a Civil War as the Southern states will leave the Union.

A picnic should end with humor, and here comes George Pickett's horse that is just about as smart as he is. This horse can't tell horse dung from oats and is tripping over his own four feet constantly! The two of them are made for each other! With all the energy George has, if he had any common horse sense, he would be scary!

A FAILURE TO COMPROMISE

This is a nation based on compromise as evidenced by conference committees assigned the tasks of wordsmith work, as well as substantive issues applied to bills coming out of the House of Representatives and the Senate. The hallmark of these legislative bodies in America has been their incredible ability to work things out for the betterment of all.

A lack of agreement has led to a war between the states in 1861. My partner, as I call Colonel Lee, has been summoned to a meeting at Blair House on April 18th with regard to the overall command of what shall later be known as "The Army of The Potomac." He has me waiting outside, but I know what his answer will be. His country is Virginia! His wife is related to Martha Washington and his father was a hero of the Revolutionary War known as "Light Horse Harry Lee." But the South is more than boundaries; it is a state of mind, and he must not draw his sword against his beloved country, Virginia. On April 20th, 1861, Colonel Lee resigns his commission from the Federal Army.

The North must look elsewhere for their leader, and Mr. Lincoln has lost his most capable soldier. So many states have left the Union that war is a reality instead of an item for fireside chats among politicians. On April 21st, 1861, the Governor of Virginia has conveyed command of the Virginia Militia to Robert E. Lee.

War is no stranger to my partner as he distinguished himself as a combat soldier in the Mexican War. On our Sunday ride, he talks to others with whom he went to West Point, knowing that they will soon be officers in a shooting war. Robert E. Lee left the Point without receiving a single demerit in his four years and was the only cadet to ever do so. The longer we are together, the more I realize this is one very special man.

No one seems to believe this is going to be more than a ninety-day war. Around the corral, our horse sense tells us this is going to be a long bloody war, and we are running a little harder and longer each day to get into battle shape. They shoot horses, too, you know!

There seem to be more generals around here than soldiers, and communications are not up to snuff. President Lincoln wants 75,000 volunteers to start with and many more to follow. President Davis asked for 100,000 men, and so many responded that one-third were sent home.

IF A HORSE COULD CRY

There is a pall over the grounds here at Arlington mansion. The family is moving out, and my partner is leaving his beautiful home to move to Richmond, Virginia. When the cherry blossoms bloom, Washington is alive with color and fragrance beyond belief. Our home and my pasture overlook the city below and are breathtaking in the spring.

The mansion is tasteful in every respect and is a two-story edifice with large white columns reaching up two stories. There is a summer kitchen not far from the main house, and I smell fried fish coming from it right now! The rooms of the house are not overdone but quite elegant, and they have served many quests of the Lee's.

The pasture is rolling in contour and lush green this time of year. I love running and mixing with the other horses. The mares have also caught my attention and are getting a little horsey. The shade trees are old and fully developed in their growth and have a certain majesty to them that is all of their own.

Wagons have come to the house for days, and all of our belongings are going in them for the journey to Richmond. My partner is sad, and while petting me, had tears in his eyes. His children were born here, and all of his memories are resting within these walls and fields of green. I have decided that it is best that I am quiet today and that I shall stay close to him when he dismounts from me. His burden is heavy and his eyes reflect that he is very tired. God bless him.

SKEDADDLE OR HORSE RACE?

Bull Run, Manassas, whatever you would like to call it turns out to be a mess. Both sides wearing the same colors shooting their own men, and at the end of the day, the Yankees looked like they were running in the Olympics back over the Potomac to Washington.

There are dead horses and men everywhere, and my partner's right arm, General Jackson, is now called "Stonewall Jackson" because of his fearless stance during the battle. The marching songs and drums are silent, and there is rust on each sword resting near a fallen soldier. Mr. McLain's summer kitchen is shot all to hell, and he is moving his family further south away from the war's path to Appomattox Court House in Virginia.

Colonel Lee has been summoned to meet with President Jefferson Davis in Richmond, and he has me on the move. Richmond, Virginia is beautiful, and the homes are truly antebellum. The ladies are dressed in multicolored dresses, and the children carry small parasols and purses. Slaves are driving carriages and serving as house servants. The horses look exceptionally groomed, and it's time for me to be at my best. Soldiers in gray uniforms salute my partner and tip their hats, but I don't think they know him.

President Davis has come out of the building to greet Bobby Lee as he calls him. He has a reputation as being one cold man, but I don't see it. His wife is a warm, sweet person who is quite attractive and likes to pat my forehead a lot. There is a great deal of respect being shown to my partner by all who meet him, and that makes me one proud horse.

General Johnston is the commanding General of the Army and is on his way to Richmond for a party in his honor. His horse is a big red guy, and they look great together.

The victory at Manassas has given everyone we meet a reason to celebrate. This undermanned army that no one thought had much of a chance has turned heads everywhere. They can fight, and their colors don't run!

THE HORNETS NEST

In April 1862, the American Civil War was accelerating with many battles. There was a large battle raging at a place called Pittsburgh Landing, and word had come here by wire that there were terrible losses on both sides. More soldiers fell in two days than in all previous American Wars put together.

My partner received word from General Beauregard that one of our best sons of the Confederacy had fallen. He was General Johnston, a great commander, and his loss had an impact on our little army, as well as on Jefferson Davis. Our President was very saddened by this event and now realized this would be a long, bloody conflict. The casualty reports showed that 30 percent of our troops who fought there were wounded or killed.

The North seemed to have also suffered a loss as General Grant had been relieved of his duties and returned to work at a desk. Someone in their War Department was working on a half bag of oats! There were reports General Grant was drunk during and after the battle. If those reports were correct, I think the Yankee War Department should have sent him cases of aged whiskey!

The battle at Pittsburgh Landing is also called Shiloh, a Hebrew word meaning a "Place of Peace." Now maybe the words should be changed to mean "Rest in Peace." The real Yankee target was the railhead at Corinth, Mississippi, but things had a way of getting out of hand in a battle scenario.

Now General Lee was concerned about commanders positioning themselves so close to the combat areas but quietly thinking some of them should run in the middle of the gunfire!

A TIME TO COMMAND

General Lee was summoned to Richmond to meet with President Jefferson Davis with only one purpose in mind, the formation of the Army of Northern Virginia under the command of General Robert Edward Lee.

The excitement over his new command was beyond belief; soldiers of all ranks believed, as the old Yankee General of the Army, Winfield "old fuss and feathers" Scott said, "Lee is the best combat officer I have ever seen." There were dissenters who called him "Granny Lee" and thought he is too old for combat command. I thought jackasses were four legged animals!

I was truly proud of this aristocrat from Virginia because he truly loved his men and cared about their welfare. His army was under clothed, under paid, under fed but very confident in their leadership and themselves. The South had limited resources in every respect except one, leadership; the South had Robert Edward Lee, who later would be recognized as the greatest general the country has ever seen.

That day it seemed like over a hundred men had touched my neck or my head after congratulating my general. Lo Armistead hugged the General, and his eyes looked moist.

He whispered in my ear, "Remember, Traveller, that glory for a horse can go away quickly; they do shoot horses." I do love that man!

General Jackson shook the general's hand and quoted some scripture to the general. A. P. Hill and his gang were there, as well as Johnston's group. Wow, what a party! In the corral, it was different than ever before. The other horses raised and lowered their heads when I walked by them.

You can't demand respect, you can only earn it, and somewhere along the way we have earned their respect.

The challenge ahead was overwhelming, but we all knew it was placed in the right man's hands.

WALTZING MCCLELLAN

We had General McClellan right where we wanted him in front of us. His target was Richmond, Virginia, and he was gathering his forces for an attack. He was called "Little Napoleon" by his troops and was very good at training but was timid about combat. Master Robert had a meeting set for that night, and some of the men were coming in.

McGruder road in to join us at the fire, along with "Old Pete" Longstreet. Pete never passed by me without rubbing my neck and saying hello. George Pickett, and of course, James "Blue Light" Jackson, who got that name because in battle his men noticed how bright his blue eyes became, along with a hoard of other officers were there to discuss how to engage McClellan's army.

Master Lee had decided that Richmond must be protected, and he needed a means for his large army to leave this area and regroup around the Richmond perimeter. There was a lot of discussion about what should be done to stop the Army of the Potomac or at least slow it down. After much discussion, it was McGruder who had a plan they all liked, but could it work? Before the war, McGruder was an actor by profession, but if he could pull his plan off, this would be his greatest part ever.

The plan was for McGruder's troops to ride in a wide circle in front of little Mac's army dragging barrels, tree limbs, anything to raise dust, while yelling and shouting commands for all to hear. This hell raising was designed to create the image of a huge force getting into position to attack. This masquerade was to last all day long and would allow my master to move the army near Richmond. It just plain worked!

Until U. S. Grant, another man from Illinois, arrived, we found General Lee outwitting commanding general after commanding general of the Army of the Potomac.

THE STORM OF BATTLE RAGES

On the general's field desk sets an engraved stone that says the following: Sometimes the Lord calms the storm, sometimes he lets the storm rage and calms the man. Together we have experienced both, and the general has never laughed so hard or cried so hard which has always been the case with the American combat soldier.

The names of these places have all run together—Chancellorsville, The Antietam, Gettysburg, and the events that took place on each battlefield are well-chronicled as they should be. Also, volumes have been written about the brilliant military strategy employed by General Lee.

Horses don't understand hate and the killing that follows. What we see is beyond horror, but there is no frame of reference other than the loss of loved ones. There is no Stonewall Jackson. Pickett's men are gone, Hill may soon die, and I have lost my dearest friend Lo Armistead at Gettysburg. Never again will he tease me but give me love at the same time.

What a horse can understand are some of the emotions of this cruel war. After Chancellorsville the General was worn out. On a hot morning, he dismounted from me and led me to an old elm tree whereupon his aids descended upon him and gave him the maps that he had requested to read. While sitting under the tree, his eyes became too much to keep open and he drifted off to sleep, dreaming of his children and Arlington. Old Pete asked that the word be passed that General Lee was asleep and to pass as quietly as possible by this position. On that day, over 15,000 men passed by without as much as a sound; they held their swords close to their bodies so as not to rattle and awaken the great man of Virginia. Most of the men who were without swords took off their hats as they so often did wherever he went. It was an unforgettable sight.

NOW THERE IS RUST ON EACH SWORD

After the surrender document was signed, numerous people in government and the military asked that Robert E. Lee lead forces against the Union to raid and prolong the conflict — he flat out refused without a shot fired.

The war is over. My general was asked to have his name placed on a company's issued certificates of insurance. The salary was enormous at over

$50,000 a year. General Lee wanted nothing to do with his name being used for commercial gain and instead accepted the position of President of Washington College for $ 1,500 per year.

He lived at the college because his Arlington home and grounds were now the nation's military cemetery, our nation's most hallowed ground. The college was well pleased with him, and old soldiers still came by and touched my saddle or rubbed my neck after they visited him. Upon his death, the college would forever be known as Washington and Lee.

Americans killed other Americans wholesale during the Civil War only to reach a point in later years where they couldn't believe it possible. I am honored to have spent those years with this nation's greatest soldier.

Chapter footnote — Traveller is the only known horse to have received full military honors upon his passing. He was buried next to Robert E. Lee, General, Commanding, The Army of Northern Virginia, and his dearly beloved friend.

He insists that Lee take his horse Traveller with him at no expense.

After the service and the obligatory visiting with the veterans in attendance, Lee manages to disengage citing fatigue. However, once Lee gives his admirers the slip, he slowly rides north towards the little town of Sharpsburg, thirty miles beyond the Potomac River.

REMEMBRANCES OF ANTIETAM

It is November 1869. R.E. Lee has come up Harper's Ferry to attend the funeral of one of his old comrades in arms, the train stationmaster near Washington College where Lee arrested insurrectionist John Brown and his followers. He was just a middle-aged colonel then, sure that fame and glory had passed him by after the Mexican-American War. He was wrong.

Splashing through the Potomac, Lee reflects on how fortunate he has been to have had such a dependable horse and companion such as nigh well inexhaustible Traveller. Carefully the big gray horse traverses through the rocky shoals to find sure footing in the swift and cold silver blue water.

As he reaches the Maryland shore, Lee turns back and reins in the great horse. His mind wanders to the memory of his men wading through these waters on their way to Sharpsburg and later Gettysburg. By the tens of thousands they came, in tattered uniforms and often barefoot. They never looked like a proper army, but as fighters, they were incomparable.

The heights about Harpers Ferry shimmer with the varied hues of the turning of the autumn leaves. Lee is reminded that the dying of the leaves signifies the drawing close of another season. Instinctively he clutches at his heart. The searing tightness of pain and the awful ache to draw air comes ever more frequent. Like the leaves and the season, Lee knows he is not long for this world. Lee does not brood on it. A man of total faith, he tranquilly accepts it as God's will.

When Lee arrives in Sharpsburg, he is not recognized. He is thinner, frailer, and aged severely by the responsibilities of war in the past decade. There is a bit of stoop to his shoulders, and his hair is now pure white. If anything he appears to be an elderly farmer gentleman.

Lee has one year left to live. On his return to Washington College, he will record these passages in his private journal:

I recall how warm it was that fall of 1862. We had whipped the Federals in the battles at Seven Pines and Seven about Richmond, badly routed Pope's legions at the Second Manassas, and seemed invincible.

The army was a mess in clothing and gear. The men were wearing out the clothes they had brought with them from home, and many had footgear with holes or were forced to go barefoot. The artillery and wagon teams' harnesses were frayed and sometimes spliced together with rope. Our logistics were thin and provisions erratic at best.

I was determined to get the Federal host out of Virginia for a spell. Already large swaths of the countryside were despoiled for farming and entire pockets of woodland denuded for firewood. I felt Virginia had suffered long enough.

President Davis even harbored hope that a victory on Federal soil could be a catalyst for foreign recognition, especially by Great Britain and France. And that would doom the Federal blockade that was beginning to cause true privation.

It was not an easy invasion. My men had been fighting virtually non-stop since May. They were tired and deserved a rest. But we had the momentum. The Federals were demoralized. I resolved to push on.

One of our big advantages in the war was that the men could easily connect with the notion of fighting for their homes and family and land. Many of the men were bothered greatly by the notion of invading the enemy. Even if, as in this case, we had thousands of Maryland troops in our ranks from that border state. They did not understand the reason was not to invade to occupy but to keep the enemy off our soil.

From exhaustion and leeriness at "invading" the enemy, I lost a quarter of the army to straggling and temporary desertion. The best entreaties of the officers and sergeants were to no avail. This was a volunteer army of amateurs mostly. So I couldn't shoot them. I knew when we returned to Virginia that they'd be there and ready to fight to defend Confederate soil. It was that kind of war.

Of course at the time, we didn't know that one of the couriers lost a copy of my order of battle circular sent to all division and corps commanders. We didn't know it fell in General McClellan's possession. We did know that "Little Mac" was moving with breathtaking speed (for him) and alacrity as if he knew our plans.

At the time, the army was badly scattered. The Federal garrison at Harpers Ferry wouldn't leave, so General Jackson had to invade the place and capture the garrison. Longstreet's corps were moving rapidly through Maryland headed for Pennsylvania.

When McClellan attacked in force against our flank division of D.H. Hill's guarding the critical South Mountain passes, I was compelled to concentrate the army and quickly. Hill barely held on in time for us to affect a concentration about Sharpsburg.

Even so A.P. Hill and his large division were still at Harpers Ferry paroling prisoners and securing the large cache of stores captured there. I had barely 40,000 men of all arms on the field, and Hill was a hard day's march away.

General Longstreet, who was cool to the invasion to begin with, strongly counseled that we withdraw behind the Potomac, which was running high. He was right that McClellan outnumbered us by three or four to one, and a loss with the river at our bank could prove calamitous.

Even combative Jackson was worried about the river. But I determined that we had to give battle to the enemy on non-Confederate soil. I knew McClellan. Even if he were moving with unaccustomed vigor, he would not get all his men in a battle if he followed his normal disposition.

What ensued was the bloodiest single day of the war they tell me. The two sides sustained over 25,000 casualties in a fairly small area. The Federals called it Antietam from the creek that formed part of our line. We called it Sharpsburg. By either name, it was a ghastly battle.

By September 1862, both armies were a far cry from the armed mobs of the previous year. The officers knew how to maneuver large masses of men. The men had absorbed massive doses of drill and actual combat experience and knew how to respond quickly and responsively to commands while under fire. Most of the incompetent and cowardly officers were gone.

The battle began early and ended late. Generally the battle was fought from left to right. Jackson's men took the first blows around the North Woods, Dunkirk Church, the East Wood, and the large Farmer Miller cornfield between them. Jackson's men blunted but could not hold back the Federal host. General Longstreet had to feed in much of his force, stripping our right flank. General Hood's division made a memorable assault to retake that terrible cornfield. The division was wrecked for the balance of the battle, and the Texas Brigade lost 82 percent of its strength in casualties. That was the most of any of my brigades in the war in a battle. For three hours and more, the battle seesawed back and forth. My boys wrecked several Federal corps.

Then the fighting shifted more to the center, and the blood ran in rivulets along the Sunken Road for over four hours. Longstreet fed in more men, and somehow we held.

Eventually the Federals on our right forced their way across the creek at the Burnside Bridge against a token force of sharpshooters. It appeared the Federals would roll forward, overwhelm our cannon on the heights about Sharpsburg, and bag the lot of us.

But then A.P. Hill came up from Harpers Ferry at forced march pace and hurled the Federals back from our right flank.

Mercifully dark fell. We had prevailed. God's will.

General Longstreet wanted immediate retreat that night. I think even Stonewall Jackson would have been glad of that, too. But I said no. I gambled that McClellan would not attack the next day, even though, true to form, he had not used all his men in the fight.

McClellan did not come. We waited a full day and then withdrew. I felt it important that we left of our own choosing and were not forced off. This was an esoteric point to Longstreet but a principled one as well to me.

Would I have embarked on that campaign in retrospect? I think so. Lincoln removed McClellan for the second and final time. The Federals would leave us alone for the balance of good weather remaining in the year.

Did we learn anything? Well, in retrospect, it reinforces the almost certain futility of direct frontal assault out in the open. It is far better to flank a foe. It reinforces the horrid consequences of standing short distances from the foe and blazing away with weapons as deadly as the rifled musket from 300 yards.

The bleak woods and fields of Antietam are a sad place, and I do not wish to visit there ever again. Too many a good man fell there for no decisive purpose.

THE RAIDERS

Both North and South knew my fame, "The Gray Ghost" is what they called me, John Singleton Mosby is my name.

As in all wars, there are characters that somehow rise to the occasion with an extreme passion for what they do best–fight! His entry into this great civil war was as a private and he exited the war as a Colonel commanding a battalion. The theater of war for Mosby was western Virginia, and his style that of a fast-striking Cavalry Raider who in the summer of 1864 may have prevented a huge Union victory, thus ending the war.

After a falling out with his commanding officer, he joined Jeb Stuart's force as a scout, and that set the stage for the legend to be born. His efforts in assisting Stuart's ride around George McClellan's Union forces during the Peninsular Campaign lead to his being granted the authority to raise a partisan force with one purpose in mind–raid!

In command of a battalion of raiders, he gave many a Yankee commander absolute fits by shooting up supply lines of all types. On one such occasion, he damn near captured the train that was occupied by General U.S. Grant himself. In order to meet this new threat, it became clear to Union commanders that they would have to divert parts of their command away from their objectives and seek out or defend against Mosby's Rangers.

In 1863 another of Mosby's exploits led him to Fairfax Court House, where he managed to awaken General Stoughton and administer a swift kick in the ass. Communication lines were a mess as the rangers captured couriers, tore down telegraph lines, and did anything and everything to disrupt the Union forces in Virginia. There was an old white church off a country road that was nestled in the woods, and like any other Sunday, services were being held there. Before the service started, a Yankee general sat in the pew and looked rather discouraged. An elderly farmer sat next to him with his young son, and they appeared to be farmers.

The farmer asked the general, "Are you okay, you look kind of glum?" The general replied that he was tired from chasing Major Mosby and that his men hadn't had a good meal in three days because that man took their supply wagons during a raid. However, the general assured the farmer that he would lay his hands on Mosby and soon! After the service, the general asked the farmer why his son had left so soon.

The farmer said, "He's not my son. That was Major John Singleton Mosby. He is a member of this church and the man you are going to catch soon!"

The Confederate Army did not convey medals or citations for excellent achievements or for leadership by its officers in battle. The most telling documents that reflect excellence were to be found in written dispatches from commanding officers. The name most mentioned for his achievements in battle in the dispatches of General Robert E. Lee, commanding General of the Army of Northern Virginia, is J.S. Mosby.

At the conclusion of the Civil War, Mosby never surrendered his regiment and instead dissolved the regiment on or about April 20th, 1865. In later chapters, we will cover in depth why the South never continued with guerrilla warfare and the immense impact such a strategy would have had for years and years to come. As in the case for many, Mosby was loyal to the Union and was a friend of US. Grant and served him in many capacities following the war.

JOHN HUNT MORGAN

John Hunt Morgan was born in Alabama, a veteran of the Mexican War with Winfield Scott, Robert E. Lee, and many others and Confederate States of America Calvary Officers. He resided in Kentucky, and between the Mexican War and the Civil War, he was a merchant in Lexington, Kentucky.

Morgan was one of the best raiders of the Civil War and without question a man to be reckoned with. Interestingly enough is the fact that Kentucky never left the Union, but Morgan sure as hell did. During the war, he held several commands, and by 1864, he commanded the departments of East Tennessee and Southwest Virginia until August 30th, 1864. He was killed in combat on September 4th, 1864.

Nathan Bedford Forrest acknowledged following the war that Morgan was highly instrumental in harassing and disrupting the Union forces, then led by Don C. Buell, that advanced on Chattanooga in 1862.

"The Long-Distance Raider" is the name we have chosen for John Hunt Morgan. Unlike John Singleton Mosby, who conducted raids on supply trains and on enemy troops near his location, Morgan was more inclined to raid all the way to Indiana. Crossing over the Ohio River in 1863 and into southern Indiana, his activities created a new type of raider that lived off the land using assets rather than destroying them. Farms that were raided provided food and water, along with grain for his men's horses; once provisioned he could then raise havoc with enemy forces. Turning to the East just outside of Cincinnati, Ohio, he instilled panic in both the military and civilian population. Fear reigned that there was a full-sized invasion force behind him. At New Lisbon, Ohio, he was finally captured and imprisoned but managed to escape in true raider fashion on November 26th, 1863. A great deal of his command was captured, but enough remained free to be an effective long-range fighting command, but with the end of the war, they disbanded.

THAT DEVIL FOREST

The fight for the Confederate granaries, arsenals, and foundries of the Tombigbee Valley, including the Battle Campaigns Q/ Okolona (January 8th, 1864-February 26th, 1864), Brice's Crossroads (June 10th-June 13th, 1864), Harrisburg (June 14th, 1864-July 23rd, 1864), and the raid on Memphis (July 24th, 1864-August 25th, 1864)

He had many names with the level of flattery or condemnation predicated on the point of view of the speaker. "Wizard of the Saddle" was a common label. Nathan Bedford Forrest was the Christian man.

Forrest was a one of a kind original and a larger than life figure. When his blacksmith daddy died, he was forced to become head of the house at sixteen. He raised his younger siblings, and from humble origins, became a successful businessman. Essentially self-taught, he spelled phonetically. But there is no doubt as to the clarity and directness of what he wrote. He was the only man in the war to enlist as a private and end it as a general. He was the only man with no formal military training to reach the rank of Lieutenant General.

His concepts of maneuver, concentration, and deception are still taught at military academies today. Even his tough foes in the western theater of the war, like Grant and Sherman, among others, candidly wrote of him as a military genius.

He was handsome, broad shouldered, tall, lean, wiry, and utterly determined. Although like almost all Southern military commanders, he opposed secession, but when it occurred, he threw himself into it totally. This occasioned the ruin of his personal fortune and massive loss of life amongst his own male relatives.

Some twenty horses would be shot out from under him. And he would personally kill at least twenty-two Federals in hand-to-hand combat. He would be wounded four times. He had no fear and would not abide a coward in his ranks.

You, the reader, should view western Kentucky, western Tennessee, northern Mississippi, and northern Alabama as essentially Forrest's Confederacy. The Federals may garrison a few places like Memphis, but the countryside belongs to Forrest. The populace is overwhelmingly with him and his men, and the Federals can make no unseen move.

At the end of the chapter, we will leave it to General Lee to muse from his private journal as to what fuller use his talents could have been applied.

While Forrest's exploits in this chapter are highly entertaining and a big blemish of Lincoln's re-election hopes in 1864, controversy rages to this day if his force could not have been better used against Sherman's supply lines in the ill-fated Atlanta campaign.

There can be no doubt that the Tombigbee Valley stretching from northeast Mississippi all the way to Mobile, Alabama was just as important to the Confederate forces of the central Confederacy as the Shenandoah Valley was to Lee's army in Virginia. Not only did it provide vast quantities of food but also the tools of war from munitions to manufactured items. It had to be defended. The controversy stems from tying down Forrest to perform that necessary defensive task.

As it was, three times Forrest will tie down, maul, humiliate, rout, and embarrass vastly superior Federal forces in the timeframe encompassed within this chapter. And this is not counting a celebrated overnight raid into Memphis.

This is not a backwater of the war. One of Grant's key objectives in 1864 was to seize Mobile—city, bay, and port and the Tombigbee Valley. Mass of force was delayed by the debacle of the ill-fated Red River expedition that diverted many of the best troops from the Vicksburg campaign of the previous year. But that will be detailed in another chapter.

The larger than life stories recounted here are true. I have taken a very few and placed them in a different point in the timeline in order to space out the humor the Forrest "Paul Bunyan" stories usually bring with them.

Remember this: Forrest's men were really mounted infantry. Erase images from your mind of cavalry sabers and plumed hats. These boys sported shotguns and pistols and weather-stained slouch hats mostly. They knew the cow paths and animal trails and they rode to get up close and flank you.

More than once the Rebels crept upon a federal garrison post and set it to flight by crashing through the tangled thickets with the cry, "Forrest is comin'! You better git!"

BRICE'S CROSSROADS

How an offense became a battle, became a defeat, became a rout, became a wholesale panic.

The column of cavalry was in a hurry but that was nothing new. If you rode with Forrest, there was generally only one speed, and that was as quick as you can. Bad weather or muddy roads made no difference.

The march was through rough, hilly country often found in northeast Mississippi. Recent rains had sliced up the narrow roads into ribbons of mud made the worse by the passage of columns of men.

General Nathan Bedford crested a small rise on his mud-splattered steed, King Phillip. Below him was an artillery caisson mired in the mud, mostly blocking the narrow road.

He drew his lithe and powerful 6'2" frame straighter, if that was possible, and scowled. His blue-gray eyes flashed with annoyance.

Captain Andrew McGregor was having a bad day. Something of a practical joker when the occasion provided as well as a full-time wit, he was exasperated with his men and himself. All their collective efforts to unstick the stubborn caisson had had the opposite effect.

Absorbed in the problem at hand, the hapless captain failed to notice Forrest bearing down on him. Thus McGregor didn't get a good look at the man other than he was obviously a general with the wreath on his collar tab of three stars.

"Who has charge here?" he demanded.

"I have, sir," answered McGregor.

"Then why in the hell don't you do something?" Forrest thundered. The general continued on in a colorful barrage of profanity.

"I'll not be cussed out by anyone, even a superior officer," retorted the chastened and angry captain. Then McGregor seized a lighted torch and abruptly thrust the flaming object into the ammunition chest–a suicidal act from the looks of it. Forrest spun around and galloped back to his staff on his hill that had been soaking in the entire episode.

"What infernal lunatic is that just out of the asylum down there?" he bellowed at his staff.

"He came near to blowing himself and me up with a whole caisson of powder!"

Forrest was answered with a chorus of laughter. Quickly his chief of artillery, Captain John Morton, let Forrest in on the joke. Some of the other men on the small hill had informed the staff that McGregor's men had already unloaded the munitions from the caisson in an effort to free it from the mud hole.

To the relief of one and all, Forrest erupted into uproarious laughter himself. Morton would later say that Forrest never cursed McGregor again.

Forrest has reason for haste. About June lst, 1864, with the authority of his departmental commander S.D. Lee, Forrest was about to embark on an expedition against Federal rail and communication lines. Forrest had received word that the Tennessee River was low and fordable, and Sherman's rail lines were guarded by second-rate troops. Everyone knew that Sherman could not sustain his large army operating towards Atlanta without the lifeline of the railroads.

The same day Forrest commenced his march for Tennessee, a Federal assault expedition was ordered by Sherman to invade northern Mississippi. Following the now familiar pattern after the fall of Vicksburg, these expeditions normally originated from Vicksburg and struck east towards Meridian or southeast from Memphis with the same object.

Burn, pillage, destroy, and raise havoc. By 1864 protection of civilian private property was a joke scarcely papered over with lip service.

Leading the Federal expedition was Brigadier General Samuel D. Sturgis, a man with a good reputation. Sturgis hailed from the West Point class of 1846. Some of his classmates were Stonewall Jackson, George McClellan, George Pickett, and a host of other good corps and division commanders in the war. He had a solid record in the War with Mexico, the Indian Wars, and in the first half of the Civil War. Sherman thought him the man to, if not to defeat Forrest outright, at least keep him at arm's length and harmless.

Sturgis sallied forth from the fortifications of Memphis with 3,300 cavalry, 5,000 infantry, twenty-two artillery pieces, and a massive train of 250 wagons. The expedition left full of bombast and bravado.

The weather declined to cooperate. After a week of rain, Sturgis called a council of war on June 8th. He stated that the streams were flooded and the roads were bad. It apparently did not occur to the council that the weather and roads presented the same problem to the Rebels. In a bad state of gloom, he offered that he feared a Confederate concentration of force if they continued on and loss of his artillery and train in the case of defeat!

A wit might argue that Federals in these parts were as afraid of Forrest as those in Virginia of Lee. Even a new man with a solid record like Sturgis seemingly was not immune from the contagion.

Fear of loss of reputation saved the day for the moment. Sturgis wrote that some of his commanders favored abandonment of the expedition, but others reminded him of Sherman's expectations and previous Federal efforts that had turned tail.

Thus a gloomy Sturgis plodded forward.

Meanwhile, Forrest was scurrying to counter the Federal host that far outnumbered his available force in the vicinity. His superior, General S.D. Lee, scurried to gather reinforcements around Tupelo and Okolona that Forrest could fall back upon if need be prior to engaging Sturgis. Lee also gave Forrest complete freedom of discretion of action and movement.

By the evening of June 9th, Sturgis had almost literally "circled the wagons" into a tight compact position about ten miles from Guntown on the Mobile and Ohio Railroad called Stubbs' Farm.

Forrest had decided to concentrate his force, too, even if it could only arrive in driblets. He wanted to keep the Federals off the railroad, block them from any further southern excursion, and defeat them.

He had to consider that Sturgis' cavalry was under the enterprising Brigadier General Benjamin Grierson, made prominent by his daring raid of 600 miles the past year from Tennessee to Baton Rouge in the Vicksburg campaign. Grierson's men had repeating carbines that gave them an awesome edge in fire superiority. The Federal infantry under Colonel William McMillen was superbly equipped and containing a black brigade that had sworn to give Forrest's men "no quarter."

On June 10th, Forrest could muster but only 4,800 men, all cavalry, save the handful manning his eight guns under the young Captain Morton and the one 100 men of his staff and escort. This would necessitate that every fourth man be detailed off as a horse holder when the battle was joined. Thus Forrest would be outnumbered by well over two to one in manpower and even more in both soldier firepower and artillery might.

Forrest's force was split among the following: Colonel Tyree Bell's Brigade mounted 2,800 while Colonels Hylan Lyon and Edmund Rucker had 750 troopers each. Also, a brigade fragment of 500 men under Colonel William Johnson arrived that day. This was all Forrest would have for several days, and he was determined to hit Sturgis hard before he could reach the railroad at Guntown. That meant holding an otherwise valueless crossroads called Brice's.

But as June the 10th dawned, only Johnson's handful was fairly near at hand. Lyon, Rucker, and Morton's eight guns were eighteen miles away, and Bell some twenty-five miles. The Sturgis column was but nine miles from the crossroads.

When June 10th dawned, it had the feel of one of those steamy summer Mississippi days when heavy rain is followed by baking sun. The sort of weather to make the stoutest man wither when subjected to strenuous exertion. In colloquial terms, a "real scorcher."

As the shards of the dawn appeared in the eastern sky, Forrest trotted up and addressed Colonel Rucker with an uncanny prediction of what would occur and what the Rebels could do to affect it.

"Edmund...I do not wish the Yankees to get astride the railroad and loot any further south in the fertile prairie country. That means we have to hold Brice's Crossroads or retake it if the Federals occupy it first."

"General, do you aim to fight with the force at hand...without Chalmers' Division and Roddey's cavalry still over in Alabama?" the brigade commander inquired.

"Yes, they can't get here in time. I grew up in large part not far from here over towards Salem. I know this terrain and this kind of weather upon it. The enemy will suffer this day."

Rucker said nothing. He glanced at Forrest's Adjutant and Chief of Staff, Major J.P.

Strange. Strange shook his head slightly and smiled as if to say, "Just listen."

Forrest continued, "I know they greatly outnumber the troops I have at hand. But the road along which they will march is narrow and muddy. They will make slow progress. The country is densely wooded and the undergrowth so heavy that when we strike them, they will not know how few men we have."

"General, this road we're on, the Wire Road, is narrower and just as muddy," Rucker noted.

Non-pulsed, Forrest expounded, "Their cavalry will move out ahead of their infantry and should reach the crossroads three hours in advance. We can whip their cavalry in that time. As soon as the fight opens, they will send back to have the infantry hurried up. It is going to be as hot as hell, and coming on a run for five or six miles, their infantry will be so tired out, we will ride right over them. I want everything to move up as soon as possible. I will go ahead with Lyon and the escort and open the fight."

With a wry glance towards Major Strange, Colonel Rucker offered, "Very well, sir, I'll hurry up my brigade as quick as I can."

"Make it quicker. As soon as we have adequate force to get on their flanks with a bulge, I want to commence putting a skeer in them!" (Note: Forrest used the term "bulge" to denote decisive force to break a line and likewise "skeer" to mean out-flanking.)

Elsewhere General Sturgis was feeling somewhat better about his prospects this morning. He reasoned the sun would lift the spirits of his men, a few days of it would dry the roads, and make the prospect of an advance down towards Tupelo more feasible. Aside from being the same age as Forrest at forty-two, his vision of the day couldn't have been more contrasting for that of Forrest.

Grierson's troopers rode off for Guntown at 5:30 A.M., but McMillan's lead brigade didn't start until 7 A.M., thus opening a real time gap between the cavalry. This also set up the basis of the scenario Forrest has just outlined on whipping the enemy cavalry and then facing the double timing and winded infantry to follow.

Grierson's cavalry began to reach the Brice's Crossroads a bit before 10 A.M. The roads led from there in three directions. One of his brigades under Waring pushed down the northeasterly choice on suspicion that the Rebels had been out that way. There they encountered a few companies of Lyon's Kentuckians under Colonel W.W. Faulkner. The Rebels cavorted in such a bold and energetic manner to throw a measure of panic in the Federals. Just as Forrest had desired and predicted.

Grierson dispatched a courier to Sturgis, who replied that a small force of cavalry should wait at the crossroads for the infantry while the balance of the troopers proceeded towards Guntown and the M & O Railroad.

Forrest had no intention of abandoning the initiative. For the first hour of the fight, he had only his escort company, Lyon's small brigade, and some odds and ends, all told not exceeding 1,000 men. He dispatched small numbers of men to charge but not in a serious manner.

"Captain Tyler," he hailed one of the more dashing of the company commanders, "I want you to push enough to confuse and puzzle them. Don't go half-cocked and get your command swallowed up. Then come back and start it all over on another part of their column. Understood?"

"Yes, sir!" Tyler drawled as he motioned at his men and rode off into the thickets.

This continued for the morning balance. Grierson reported, "Three desperate attempts to take our position." The cavalryman stated he was in an advantageous position if the infantry could be rapidly brought up. Sturgis directed McMillan to bring up his men as "rapidly as possible without distressing them," and rode forward for a look.

What Sturgis found was a narrow causeway almost a mile long across a flooded lowland leading to a narrow bridge across flooded Tishomingo Creek.

"My God!" he exclaimed to an aide. "This place is already jammed with artillery and ambulances! Find an officer to clear the road for the infantry at once."

Arriving at the crossroads, Sturgis found Grierson's two brigade commanders in near panic and wanting relief or the order to retire. Grierson himself was more sanguine and non-committal on his prospects. Sturgis immediately ordered the infantry to "lose no time coming up."

By 1:00 P.M., Grierson was asking for his entire force to be taken from the line. His troopers had fired their new repeaters with little or no fire discipline into the woods and the thickets at the noises designed by the Rebels to cause that very action. As a result, the Federal cavalry was virtually out of ammunition!

Colonel McMillan rode up the crossroads at this point in advance of his lead infantry brigade and exclaimed to Sturgis, "General, looks like everything is going to the devil as fast as it possibly can."

Tossing prudence aside just as Sturgis and the Federal cavalry commanders before him, he ordered his two lead brigades to come ahead at the double quick (or steady trot) before the Federal perimeter collapsed.

Meanwhile, Forrest had placed Lyon aligned along the Wire Road with Rucker and Johnson in on the left and right as they showed up. Unlike the panicked Federals, Forrest knew the two Federal cavalry brigades overlapped his flanks and they had artillery while he had none.

"Major Anderson!" he barked to his Assistant Adjutant General. "Charles, ride hard to Bell. Tell him to move up fast and fetch all he's got. And hurry up Morton's guns, too!" Anderson nodded and spurred away towards Booneville and Reinzi.

McMillan's unnecessary order had taken the last of the vigor out of the exhausted Federal infantry. Those who didn't succumb to heat exhaustion or stroke were clearly winded, blown, and in great distress.

Although the fighting had been desperate and at times at close quarters, the Rebels had won the feint and bluff portion of the battle. Now a quiet lull settled over the field and the Federal cavalry withdrew. The sweating infantry tried to gather their energy and deploy and the Rebels waited on their main battle force.

General Abraham Buford, a West Pointer Division Commander, arrived on the field. Forrest assigned him command of the three brigades on the right and placed Bell's brigade on the left as it came up along with Morton's guns.

Shortly after Forrest ordered the first true Confederate attack of the day as the main battle phase opened. Riding the lines with saber in hand after conferring with Bell, Forrest shed his officer jacket and fought with rolled up sleeves in the sweltering heat.

As he moved through the dismounted troopers in the thickets, he alternately explained, encouraged, cursed, praised, demanded, and occasionally threatened to shoot any man afraid of the Yankees.

Captain Morton's position was paid a special visit.

"Morton, I want you to double shot your guns with canister. When the bugle sounds on the left, Bell's men will charge, and I want you to go in with them keeping pace. Ignore your flanks. The advance will take care of that."

Dumbfounded the Captain was rendered speechless.

Over and over, Forrest repeated, "Get up, men. I have ordered Bell to charge on the left. When you hear his guns and the bugle sounds, every man must charge, and we will give them hell."

It was a nasty affair of a charge through the brambles, stickers, and thick brush of blackjack and brushwood. Bell's brigade slammed head on into the second Federal infantry brigade on the field, which stood fast and even briefly gave pursuit after an initial repulse. Forrest had to fling his own escort into the sortie with pistols blazing to fling the Federals back. Meanwhile, over on the right, Buford had his hands full as he tangled with the first Federal infantry brigade to arrive.

In such frequent close quarters, weapons became clubs once discharged, and there was considerable hand-to-hand fighting. Finally, by around 4:00 P.M. as Forrest listened to the ebb and flow of battle, he judged "by ear" that the time had come to take matters to a climactic level.

"Bring me Lieutenant Cowan of my escort," Forrest ordered to Major Strange. When Strange produced the smoke darkened George Cowan, Forrest grabbed his arm in an animated fashion and shouted above the din, "Hit 'em on the e-e-eend!" This was the traditional Forrest-speak for flank and envelope the enemy.

"With what, General?" replied the practical young officer. "We're thin as hell now."

"They don't know that. Those Yankees are primed for a stampede. Take the escort and Captain Tyler's Kentuckians."

Shortly thereafter, on the extreme left, the little force of about 250 Rebels got beyond the Federal right and thinly deployed themselves into the Tishomingo Creek bottoms and created maximum racket and mayhem. As icing Forrest's redoubtable bugler Jimmy Bradford galloped along the line sounding the charge at spaced intervals to create the illusion of an advancing host. The illusion of strength was well done, unnerving the Federal ranks and sowing doubt.

Judging the battle at the apex he had dreamed up that dawn, Forrest hurriedly gathered his staff.

"Now is the time, boys!" he raged. "Strange, find Buford and tell him to press them. Press in and on." Dr. Cowan, his wife's cousin and medical director, was told to order Morton to push forward and range the Federal bottleneck at the Tishomingo Creek Bridge. "Shell 'em hard," he thundered. To Major Stevenson, his Quartermaster, he screamed, "Tell Bell the enemy will have to thread the needle under cannon fire...tell him to move in and get goin'! Now!" Finally he told his personal aide and son, Willie Forrest, and Chaplain Colonel Kelly to follow him close with "pistols at the ready."

The combined effects of the advance began to germinate the desired results. Gradually the Federals fell back in increasing disorder. By 5:00 P.M. the Federal force was quitting the field and leaving the crossroads. Federal officers made repeated attempts to reform the lines, but the Rebels pressed too hard to stem the withdrawal, which was becoming a rout.

As the Federals fled past the two-story Brice house, they sought shelter by retracing their steps back down the road that they had marched up hours earlier. The result was a bottleneck under cannon fire, not only from

Morton's guns but four abandoned Federal pieces Morton's men commandeered and turned on the late owners.

Facing the creek bottom and the narrow rail less Creek Bridge, the bluecoat rout degenerated into a scene worthy of Dante's Inferno. Inevitably a laden wagon turned over on the bridge and blocked the way. The Federal host piled up on the bridge approach. To the sides were the swollen creek bottoms. Ahead was the bottomland along the narrow causeway. Pandemonium broke out. A snarled mass of caissons, ambulances, and artillery corked the bridge approaches.

Men began to try to cross in the neck deep water and wade across while under fire. Some drowned while others were shot down from all sides as Forrest's escort, and Tyler's men fired at them with harassing fire from the other side of the creek.

About the only thing that slowed the Rebels was the sight of abandoned provision wagons. Many of the ever-hungry Rebel force stopped to grab Federal hardtack or slabs of bacon that they devoured raw and then moved on.

The third and final battle phase, the pursuit had commenced. It would continue until the Federals were hounded all the way back to Memphis, over seventy miles away.

Meanwhile, Sturgis' third infantry brigade, the black outfit under Colonel Bouton, had been guarding the large wagon train parked in a field by the creek bottoms. It was decided to attempt to turn it around and retrace the route back to Memphis. However, it is no small task to turn around over 200 wagon teams in the midst of a stampede and a jammed road. Officers jockeyed for road access for their units and material.. .the artillery wanted to pass ahead and confusion was the result. With the flotsam and debris of the battle surging back on the trains, all efforts to salvage most of the train were abandoned in the ensuing hours.

Some teamsters attempted to burn their wagons, and many cut the traces and took off on the horses and mules to the rear post-haste.

Sturgis lamented to everyone and no one in particular as he railed about the "uncontrollable panic."

He announced the artillery and the train "gone to hell" and asked Cavalry Brigadier Winslow to attempt to shield the stampeding force after it passed his force.

Colonel Bouton implored Sturgis, "General, for God's sake, don't let us give up so." For the moment, Sturgis was quite unhinged.

"What can we do?" he wailed.

Over Rebel way, Forrest drummed the non-stop order, "Keep the skeer on 'em!" In typical Forrest fashion, he now considered the Federal wagons "his" and railed at his men to save the burning wagons, where some of his troopers had stopped to admire the eerie conflagration.

"Don't you see the damned Yanks are burning my wagons?" he raged. "Get off your horses and throw the burning beds off!" More afraid of Forrest than the piles of burning bacon and hardtack, the men formed into teams and heaved the burning beds off the wagon's chassis.

Along the raggedly surging line, the "Rebel Yell" burst forth from here and there, thicket to thicket, as dusk settled in. Like an accordion, it flowed left to right and right to left. The men had been part of something greater than themselves. And they knew it.

Eventually even the redoubtable Forrest knew his exhausted men had to rest. Most had rode hard eighteen to twenty-five miles that day, fought hard, and were awfully hungry and sleep famished. Employing his usual pursuit tactics, he continued on with smaller advance forces to harass the enemy.

"Major Strange, order the main body to hold up, rest, and eat. Tonight every man is his own commissary sergeant. Tell the men to eat their fill and take all they can on their persons and horses for the next several days' rations," Forrest said softly as he lapsed into his normal soft non-battle mode of speech.

"Gladly, sir," replied the begrimed Strange, who sported a grin in a voice half-choked with Federal hardtack himself.

"Quartermaster Severson, at first light commandeer all the lightly wounded, unhorsed men and the like and sort all this mountain of supplies. I want no waste!"

"Willie, find General Buford. Tell him his men are to form a provost guard. He is to round up and guard the prisoners, which it appears we will have in large numbers at first light and the next few days. But tell him to be ready to move quickly with most of his men as circumstances dictate."

Meanwhile, the hapless Colonel Bouton prevailed upon the dispirited Sturgis to provide him ammunition and some of the white troops to form with his black troops to try and extricate the wagons and uncaptured artillery.

"For God's sake, if Mr. Forrest will let me alone, I will let him alone."

Nathan Bedford Forrest had absolutely no intention of that. He renewed the pursuit about 1:00 A.M. and reached the Federal cavalry rear guard about 3:00 A.M. About three miles from the battlefield, the road crossed the bottomland of one of the headwater streams of the Hatchie River. It was here that the surviving wagons and artillery became hopelessly bogged down in a slough filled with muck and mud. Forrest bagged the balance of the wagons and another fourteen field pieces.

Onward through a muggy and shower-filled night, the ever more miserable Federals plodded back the way they had come. Even more shed themselves of weapons, ammunition, equipment, and accoutrements of soldiering. Some dispirited Federals gave up the retreat and found a handy log or tree limb that provided some small measure of dryness relative to the boggy landscape.

Small cadres of Forrest's troopers cut into the ranks of the retreating Yankees. On occasion they picked men off and claimed them as prisoners less their food, gear, and of course, horses.

A dejected Federal trooper remarked to one rider coming up beside him in the darkness, "Old Forrest gave us hell today!" He then went on to estimate Forrest's host as 50,000 men and stated the woods were "full of 'em." Suppressing a laugh, his fellow rider produced a Colt revolver, shoved it into the man's rib cage, and informed him that he, too, was now a prisoner of one of "Old Forrest's men."

Nearing his boyhood home of Salem, even the fatigue-less Forrest fell sound asleep as trusty King Phillip carried him along. Private Mack Watson of Forrest's Escort Company noticed this and reported the predicament to his commander, Captain Jackson.

"Go wake him up, Mack," was the response.

"No, sir, you go wake him!" prudently answered the private.

"Tell Colonel Bell," was the revised order.

"Ride ahead and wake him up, Mack!" directed Bell..

While this caution towards Forrest's occasional temper was playing out, evidently an equally weary King Phillip drifted off the road and brushed Forrest into a tree, unhorsing him with an abrupt wake-up call.

Problem solved.

Presently Forrest told Watson to double back and tell General Buford to "gallop up."

On receipt of the message, exhausted Buford exclaimed, "Tell General Forrest, by God, that my men can't gallop up."

Watson started back when he heard the bugle sound from Buford's bugler calling the column to gallop. Even General Buford did not care to fool with Forrest's ire, weary or not.

About four miles short of Ripley, as dawn broke, the Rebels encountered a feeble rear guard minus any desire to fight. Jubilant Confederates drove them through town. The Federals reinforced and tried again and scattered for good.

Ripley Forrest placed the direct pursuit with Buford, who pushed too hard for Forrest to swing around via another route with Bell's brigade and snare the entire lot.

No real harm done there. The Federal spirit was so broken that they could scarcely be stopped short of Memphis.

As it was, Forrest had his hands full gathering the fugitives in from the chase, sorting out the spoils, and resting his worn-out mounts and men.

This did not cause the Yankees to desist in the wholly unfounded fear that Forrest was upon them and at their flanks until Memphis was reached.

It was a smashing victory. One of the few times in the war that an army had been beaten, induced to wholesale panic, utterly defeated mentally, and unburdened of almost all of its means of waging war.

The advance had taken more than a week. The vanquished Federals made the return seventy-mile trip in a night, a day, and a night. The final leg was by special train excursions run out to pick up survivors.

Forrest's haul was eighteen guns, almost 200 wagons, 1,500 rifles, 300,000 rounds of small arms ammunition, priceless medical supplies, numerous horses and mules, and enough equipment and food to re-equip much of his force and feed them for weeks. Sturgis lost 617 casualties, and Forrest captured another 1,600 more. Perhaps as many again Federals deserted and made their way back home or became armed lawless hoodlums or "bummers." Forrest lost no material and sustained 492 in losses of all types. And the productive Tombigbee Valley was unscathed.

Forrest was generous in praising the mettle of his foe. He reported that while they chose to fight, they fought well.

Finger pointing and acrimony set in immediately on the blue side. Cavalry and infantry commanders blamed the other service and hurled out uncomplimentary names and expletives towards each other. And everyone blamed Sturgis, too. Many accused Sturgis of being drunk, which was not true.

Sturgis was sacked of course and saw no more assignments for the balance of the war. His next assignment was as a garrison commander in Austin, Texas in post-war Texas in the summer of 1865.

Sturgis was certainly especially ill-served by his cavalry commanders. But with his training and experience, he should have known better than to walk into the snare of an almost obvious ambush on the other side of that long causeway across the narrow creek bridge and to the thickets beyond. This was a poor disposition with no easy exit, even in dry terrain.

A disappointed but reflective "Crump" Sherman mused over the debacle. He reasoned that he had at least kept Forrest's men off his rail lines for a few more weeks. Sherman was already planning another move towards him on receipt of the news. Forrest and his men would have little rest.

One of the few charming things about Sherman was his gift for writing both as he thought and spoke. He pinned perhaps his most famous lines, and that from a prolific and gifted writer, "I will order them to go out and follow Forrest to the death if it costs 10,000 lives and breaks the Treasury." There will never be peace in Tennessee until Forrest is dead...

Excerpt from General Lee's private journal, 1867:

"I knew the efforts of General Forrest in the spring and fall of 1864 in only the most general terms. I learned a bit more when I became commander-in-chief of Confederate forces in February 1865. But it is only after the war that I became privy to a deeper understanding of the man, his men, and their accomplishments.

There is no doubt in my mind that he had to be a natural genius for war both strategically and tactically. Some men become good as organizers and trainers, others are wonderful with logistics, others fight a great battle the length a field he can see, and still others have the insight to plan. Forrest clearly could do all those things and more. And I say this without the benefit of having met and visited with him.

He used his cavalry in a more muscular way, if that is the proper term, than our other cavalry commanders. Jeb Stuart, Earl Van Dorn, Joe Wheeler, John Morgan, and the rest were more traditional patrol, raid and fight the opposing cavalry style leaders. Forrest was the only cavalry leader we had that could not only destroy the enemy railroads lines for long periods of time but on occasion completely render lines utterly useless for the balance of the war.

I do not know if General Forrest could have effectively managed a much larger force, but I suspect so. He seems in retrospect as something of a cavalry version of a Stonewall Jackson. His men loved the results he got out of them but also feared him, too.

President Davis was right to want to protect the Tombigbee Valley and Mobile in 1864. But he was wrong to assign Forrest to that task. While Forrest did siphon off troops that otherwise were scheduled to go to Sherman in his Atlanta campaign, it was a waste of talent.

I know now that at times Sherman ran low on supplies against Johnston. With Forrest astride his railroad lines, Atlanta may have been held with Johnston still in command further north of that point, and Lincoln may have lost the presidential election.

It was a costly, perhaps fatal mistake on the part of President Davis."

EVE OF THE CAMPAIGNS OF 1864

The illusions of both sides were mostly dissipated by early 1864. War had scarred the landscape and American mental state to an undreamed of level of carnage and waste.

The past speeches of the politicians and orators rang hollow. The war had a veritable life of its own. Only fools spoke gaily of gallantry and sacrifice, and typically they weren't the ones being shot at or called on to bear the suffering.

Loss of life had reached undreamed of proportions. Kentucky, Missouri, and large swaths of Arkansas, Tennessee, Mississippi, Louisiana, Virginia, and the ocean side of the Carolinas had felt the hard hand of Federal army occupation and destruction. The Mississippi River corridor was occupied by the Federals, and the Confederacy chopped into a main portion and the westerly Trans-Mississippi region.

Yet, after almost three bloody years of fighting, the core of the Confederacy was still intact with willpower, military power, and infrastructure. Dissatisfaction with the Lincoln administration was very high in the North. Union draft dodging, draft riots in the cities, and considerable desertion was the result in 1863.

The matter was coming down to matter of purpose, will, and tolerable degree of suffering. Federal purpose was more intangible. Fighting to "preserve" the Union with a South that wanted no such thing was an increasingly hard sell to the Federal veterans who had witnessed much death far from home. And save for some idealistic New England regiments, few Yankees gave a tinker's damn about slavery or blacks one way or another. But the Federals had a big plus on their side of the ledger, too. They didn't have to worry about their homestead being burned and their family and old folks left to starve or their women violated. If you could ignore the danger and dismiss the suffering you inflicted on civilians, war was still an adventure, although of the hard-bitten variety.

Confederates had the advantage of defending their home ground and families. And through the hardships of the first part of the war, they had learned how to make do with less and become accustomed to always being outnumbered. From this they drew a defiant and sardonic espirit de corps that sustained most of them.

It was a large war with large numbers of men. As Rebel regions were over-run and the pitiful letters from home reached the men, some could handle the strain no more. Confederate desertions increased as men crept away to serve in "home guard" or "militia" units that did little good other than harass the populace for food and goods. Others became out and out bandits. The social fabric of the South was straining and tearing at the seams.

In the harsh winter of 1863 to 1864, a massive religious revival spontaneously broke out amongst all Confederate armies and the civilian population, too. As the war turned ever more vicious, Southerners of all classes implored God to save them from the invaders and give them strength.

By early 1864, the creaking Confederate railroads still moved supplies and troops over worn rails with tired equipment. Indeed the confederates were writing the book on using modern interior lines of supply and communication as they went along. Over one in two blockade-runners made it into port or beached on shore in high tide to have goods offloaded. The absence of so many men in the armies impeded the efforts to supply soldiers with foodstuffs, but enough got through to sustain the increasingly emaciated Confederate troops. Goods of all types were in short supply. Simple essential things like cloth, shoe wear, sewing needles, basic medicines, and salt were worth more than a handful of gold coins. However, the munitions armament complex nestled in the Confederate interior supplied ample stocks of ammunition and arms of all types. So far the Federals had failed to damage confederate efforts to produce the means of war.

What couldn't be denied was that the South was worn. The countryside and town and cities looked it. The Reb soldiers were generally in tattered garments, and many were barefoot. The armies though were still defiant. The soldiers were mostly veterans now. They knew the measure of their better-supplied foe and figured they had the stronger will to endure another year. Nobody expressed the opinion that one smashing battle would win the war. The killing power of both sides almost precluded the destruction of a large opposing force. The soldiers were much quicker on the uptake on that reality than some of their generals who learned war in theory by study of the Napoleonic Wars earlier in the century. The rifled musket and improved cannon had changed that forever.

Vicksburg had fallen. Lee's second invasion of the North was a second failure at Gettysburg. Chattanooga had fallen. The confederate counter-thrust victory at Chickamauga in the fall of 1863 was squandered by Davis' pet, General-Braxton Bragg. Galveston, Texas was re-taken in a Christmas 1863 surprise present, and there were local successes against the Federals in the Carolinas. Lee and Meade had fumbled at each other in an unsatisfactory half-hearted effort in the fall of 1863 Mine Run campaign by two armies just too weary after Gettysburg and the gore that preceded it.

Year 1864 was an election year. It seems so evident now from afar through the prism of almost 150 years of time that a new dynamic was at play. The South could not and did not need to "win." It had only to prevail in 1864 with no major mistakes, and the unhappy electorate might boot the Lincoln administration out of office.

Certainly the rank and file knew it, as well as many of the Confederate generals. However, President Davis, inflexible with his micro-managing department strategy of defending everything, did not see it. He did hear the pleas of local politicians and minor local generals that played up the importance of their locale. Turning a deaf ear to the need of concentrating to hold the key points to deny the Federals any significant physiological victories, he made the task harder than it already was.

The Confederacy had a secretary of war, but Davis was really his own and his own chief of staff, too. By interfering with the Confederate military leadership, which was still as good if not better than the Federal, he neglected his political role of leadership in economics, public morale, monetary and fiscal policy, and general administration.

Meanwhile, out of the Vicksburg campaign came Grant, who Lincoln gave virtual carte blanche to run the military. With his old sidekick Sherman and sundry lesser lights, they devised a war scheme of total warfare against the Confederate civilian population. Lincoln acquiesced to this shift of policy. They even stopped the highly humane and supremely honorable prisoner exchange program to which both sides had faithfully abided saving hundreds of thousands from the suffering of long-term imprisonment and likely death in the ghastly prisoner camps of the time. Confederate protests fell on cold deaf ears. Although the Yankee prisoners received the same meager ration as Confederate troops, the close confinement would doom tens of thousands to death from sickness and poor sanitary conditions of being held in close quarters. Yet those rations were deprived of the Rebel armies. This was total war.

As the cards were reshuffled for the campaigns of 1864, there were some changes. Faced with a near mutiny of the leadership and rank and file of the long-suffering Army of Tennessee, Davis reluctantly removed the incompetent Bragg to be his personal "military advisor." The army commander replacement was the ever-popular Joe Johnston, who Davis had despised since West Point.

Perhaps more so than any other senior Confederate leader, Johnston saw it all clearly and strategically. If he could hold Atlanta against the campaign surely coming from Sherman until November's elections, if Mobile stood fast, and if Lee held Richmond, the war weary Northern public might just do the job and end this war.

While General Lee began an increasingly blunt letter writing campaign to badger Davis for more men, especially his own units, Davis had scattered across the landscape, and Johnston set about quickly restoring the morale and logistics of the Army of Tennessee.

Ahead lay the first full year of total war in American history with all the attendant barbarity such a policy implied.

CLARK MOUNTAIN, VIRGINIA

SUNDAY AFTERNOON
MAY 1st, 1864

It had been a rainy April in Central Virginia. Now the tree leaves and grass were turning green, and the wildflowers were out in profusion. Clark Mountain was one in name only for the isolated highpoint of some 1,100 feet provided a crow's nest view of the area. This was especially the purpose of the Confederate signal station situated there. Down below off the northwest was The Wilderness region. It was there that the great battle of Chancellorsville had been fought with the loss of Stonewall Jackson muting the Confederate victory almost a year ago.

That morning Lee had sent word for First Corps Commander Pete Longstreet to meet him for a talk at the station on the mountain. Longstreet was told to come alone. Since Longstreet's men were a day's march away at Gordonsville guarding the Virginia Central Railroad, Lee intended to arrive some time ahead of him and do some private thinking.

"Colonel Taylor!" Lee barked as he emerged from his headquarters tent. Lee's adjutant turned his head up from the table where he was focused on the unending paperwork of an army, even in camp.

"Have Traveller saddled. I'm meeting General Longstreet at Clark Mountain as you know, and I do not wish to be disturbed at all barring some calamity. Assign me no more than two of your couriers as escorts."

"Yes, sir!" Taylor replied. As he hurried away, Taylor wondered what the meeting was for, but the "Old Tycoon," as he called Lee behind his back, had been tight lipped about it, and like the devoted aide he was, he asked no questions.

Looking about in the sunshine of the day, Lee could see the line of supplicants held back respectfully by the headquarters' guards seeking audience with him. He sighed. Every day they came with some seeking favor of one sort or another. Others wished to complain of the lack of food, clothing, and footwear. He was glad to leave these thankless chores to his staff officers. He had weightier matters on his mind. He put on his stained travel gloves.

An orderly brought forward seven-year-old Traveller, who was moving along with his usual springy step. The mid-size gray horse with the black tail was almost prancing its small feet forward.

Lee smiled and accepted the reins, tickling the horse's small delicate ears. Lee had other horses, but this one was his favorite, particularly for days like this. As he mounted with the grace of a man who spent decades in the saddle, his two escorts came up and saluted.

Lee nodded and set off, the cavalrymen falling in behind. Traveller wasn't the easiest horse to ride, but Lee made it look easy as he rode forward at a smooth easy canter.

Presently Traveller was guiding the way up the familiar mountain path. He had been here with Lee often the past few months and knew the way, requiring little rein work by Lee. The horse was pleased to carry its master on these rides. While he knew he was Lee's favorite, he was also mindful Lee rode the others to avoid burning off his horseflesh. Even a commanding general's horse often got minimal fodder for subsistence. Central Virginia was about played out for supporting horses and mules. Traveller knew he was lucky to get as much corn to eat as he did.

As Lee reached the eminence, the dozen or so men of the signal station waved and grinned. They knew Lee enough to not be over awed by his presence.

The sergeant in charge saluted and took the reins as Lee dismounted. Lee returned the salute and pulled his field glasses from his saddlebags.

"Any change, Sergeant?" he softly asked.

"No, sir. Same as before. The enemy camps continue to stir as they prepare to break winter quarters. No move towards the fords yet, though I suggest that will be sooner than later."

"Yes, I think perhaps this week. I know you will continue your vigilance. General Longsreet will join me later in the afternoon. Just ignore us and go about your duties. I may ask to borrow your spy glass later," Lee responded as he retrieved his field glasses.

"Yes, sir. Do we let Traveller graze about unattended as usual?"

"Yes. He's too curious about my doings to wander off!" Lee laughed gently.

The sergeant removed the bridle and saddle and left the General and his horse to their own devices.

Traveller inwardly smiled for he enjoyed the intimate conversations only he was privy to with Lee and the senior commanders.

As his horse grazed on the fresh grass, Lee eyed a group of logs and stumps the men had arranged around a campfire that now burned low.

Lee sat down on a stump and felt a slight stirring tugging about his heart. He silently prayed a brief appeal for strength to not fail him in the coming campaign. Superbly conditioned throughout his life as a soldier, it was only the previous year when his health had begun to afflict him. A man of iron control, he was frustrated to the point of expiration over the deterioration of his physical self. Only a few of his staff and the doctors knew the depth of how his heart problems were an increasing concern. Outwardly he had aged rapidly in this war, and his hair had turned from brown to gray with white now spreading about his temples.

A devout Episcopalian, he stoically accepted his fate and God's will and did not fear death for himself. He did, however, fear very much any inability to do his duty for he was a strong man of conviction and principle.

Glancing about to make sure he was alone, he gathered his thoughts. Silent for some moments, he was only vaguely aware that he was speaking softly. Only Traveller could hear his thoughts almost enunciated in a whisper.

"We can't win now in a Napoleonic way. Those days are gone. With modern firepower, communication, and railroads, it is impossible to destroy an army for either side if the commander hasn't any skill at all. This can't go on. We've lost so many of the best officers and tens of thousands of the best troops. The Federals can replace their losses with ease, and we cannot. And our infrastructure is strained to the point of collapse. If we are forced to a permanent defensive, then it must be for a purpose. General Longstreet will like that."

Did I make a mistake in insisting on the campaign that led to the defeat at Gettysburg? When President Davis ordered me to meet with him and his cabinet after Chancellorsville, I spent two days in Richmond stubbornly arguing for my plan. My debate point that the Mississippi heat was too intense for Grant to capture Vicksburg looks ludicrous now. Only Postmaster General Reagan of Texas took me to task over it.

Yet I prevailed with that command presence I was born to, coupled with my track record. What would have happened if I had taken Longstreet's Corps and assumed command personally against this man Grant before he encircled Vicksburg?"

Lee shook his head. Head bowed and lost in thought, he said nothing for some time.

Murmuring softly again, he opined, "Am I to wed to Virginia with my personal preference to serve here? Should I have taken over from Bragg after he spoiled Longstreet's great Chickamauga victory by doing nothing? I turned the President down again. And then the Federals took Lookout Mountain that seems impossible from afar here. I can't dwell on it though. Now Grant is here before us in command of all their armies, but he will attach himself to Meade, so I know who's really directing their campaign in Virginia. And unlike all my previous foes, I don't know the man. I can't even recall his face from the War of 1848, but I must have met him."

Lee turned and glanced at Traveller, who was standing very close now. The great horse nuzzled his shoulder as if in empathy, and Lee idly patted the horse's head.

They were thus for some time when the sound of horse hooves came wafting up the path to the station. Lee stood up and saw General Longstreet approaching with a couple of escorts behind.

They had not seen each other in some eight months, and so much had happened since Lee sent his "Old War Horse" and his corps to fight what became the great Confederate victory at Chickamauga south of Chattanooga.

Lee smiled with genuine affection as the big burly man approached. To most the brushy bearded blue-eyed Georgian appeared to be the slowish, uncomplicated physical type of General. Lee knew better for he was a complex intellect not visible on the surface.

Eyes growing misty, Lee exclaimed, "Pete, I am so glad to see you and have looked forward to this for so long!"

Longstreet grinned and saluted. Dismounting heavily he motioned his escort away with his horse.

As Lee returned the salute, Longstreet extended his hand that Lee quickly shook firmly. Both men gazed briefly in one another's eyes and then spontaneously grabbed each other briefly in a soldier's hug. That display of emotion was out of character for both, and each looked a little sheepish. Then they both laughed.

Lee motioned Longstreet to sit, and they sat down on the log stumps.

"I'm damn glad to be back to the Army of Northern Virginia, General Lee. I'm glad to be back home."

Lee nodded. "God knows you're needed here. Tomorrow I will summon all the corps and most of the Division Commanders to this very place. I want to explain to them my plans so far as I can develop them for the campaign ahead. But first I wanted to see the Deputy Ccommander of this army in private."

Longstreet listened intently and pulled out his pipe, which he filled and lit with a Lucifer match striking against his battered boot.

I hope my health will prevail in good stead in the months ahead. But if it does not or if I'm injured, you must take over. So you must know my plans if you should come to serve in my stead.

Longstreet's eyebrows arched up slightly, and he nodded.

"Only my staff knows this, and I take you in my confidence. My heart has increasingly proved troublesome. I can't follow the advice of the doctors to take it easy. I do not fear death, as you don't. Consequently I must insist, must order, that you stay well back of the battle line. I can't afford to lose you. There is no other officer present capable of leading the army. Promise me, Pete."

"General Lee, I'll try, but battles are fluid with the ebb and flow against a larger foe. Still I will try to do my best," Longstreet offered.

"Very well. Now before proceeding on the matters at hand, I wish to hear of your campaigns out west in your own words. I've read the reports, but I know too well they rarely tell all."

"First, sir, I must tell you the troops out there are just as good as ours and the officers, too. The poor Army of Tennessee has really suffered. They began the war under Albert Sidney Johnston, who lost Kentucky and most of Tennessee and then lost Shiloh under first the now-late Johnston and then Beauregard. Then most of them served under Bragg in the Perryville campaign that amounted to nothing and a standoff battle at Stone's River. Then Bragg managed to let himself get maneuvered out of middle Tennessee and lost Chattanooga, too.

Then my corps and some other reinforcements arrived last fall, and we whipped the Yankees very badly at Chickamauga. Bragg played no part. The generals out there tell me his style is to simply order attack from the left or right echelon and then detach himself too far back to even know what's happened. He has no tactical or strategic skill. The men hate him and most of the officers, too. Even worse they have no respect for him. He's a professional martinet with logistical skill, sort of a McClellan with no fighting ability." Longstreet paused and gazed at Lee, who sat stoically.

"Go on, General."

"Sir, forgive the harsh words, but I do not exaggerate. Bragg is one of Davis' pets like Pemberton was, and if you find fault with those types, the President takes it as a personal insult. Well, after the victory at Chickamauga, Bragg wouldn't exploit it and settled into a silly semi-siege of Chattanooga. The rank and file were in an uproar, and a petition of many of the officers was sent to the President. He came himself and saw and heard the complaints in person. President Davis then called a meeting of all the senior officers with Bragg present. The president asked me if Bragg should be removed, and I told the truth. I said 'yes' in no uncertain terms.

I could see in the President's eyes; he was angry with me. He'll harbor anger towards me to eternity. Then I was sent off by Bragg to try to pry Burnside out of Knoxville but mainly to dispense of my unwelcome presence. Knoxville is unshakeable with superb defenses versus my two divisions. I had to try one effort and maybe induce Burnside to come out and take me on, but he wisely just sat still. I heard that Grant was dispatching Sherman's men to come up in my rear, so my only course was to cross over the mountains and return to Virginia.

Then came the battles for Lookout Mountain. Grant had brought up a lot of fresh troops to relieve Chattanooga and a big bunch of his troops from the Vicksburg operation, too. Somehow Bragg lost what they call "The Battle of the Clouds." Evidently Bragg placed his men on the exact military slope instead of the true slope, so that the men couldn't shoot down at the attackers, and panic ensued. If Pat Cleburne's fine division hadn't held the Yankees off, much of Bragg's army may have been destroyed. After that I hear that the men were catcalling Bragg derisive names in such numbers, he could not try to begin to .hoot or hang them.

So Davis had to remove Bragg or face a near-mutinous army. As you know, he made that worthy his Chief Military Advisor. That means he'll be free to meddle in Johnston's affairs as his replacement. He'll likely try to meddle in yours, too," Longstreet said with a touch of sarcastic bitterness.

Neither spoke for a moment. The amplification was no surprise to Lee really but stung just the same.

"Pete, I know you won Chickamauga, not Bragg. When the President came out to visit, is it true he offered you the army command after you said Bragg must go?" Lee asked earnestly.

"Yes, sir, and I declined immediately. That displeased him, too. Then he asked whom I would choose. Then I said Joe Johnston of course. Davis looked furious. I think my stock with the President and the War Department is pretty low."

"General, such offers come rarely. I'm somewhat surprised you declined. Care to elaborate for me?" Lee asked with great curiosity.

Sir, if, God forbid, you became incapacitated, I feel confident I could take over the Army of Northern Virginia and do a fairly credible job. I know the people, your organization, and the terrain. But the poor hapless Army of Tennessee is riddled with factions, and I would be new to them as a first time Army Commander. You told me once that the leap from one command level to the next is vast. I've learned a lot the past eight months. I have to subordinate my ambitions for what is best for the greater good. General Johnston is a good man, a full General with experience as an army and theater commander. In that last role, he was Bragg's nominal boss part of last year and visited the army often. He knows the personnel of the army pretty well and is popular with the army, too," Longstreet explained in a soft, forthright voice.

Lee said nothing for a moment and then replied, "Pete, I'm touched. I truly am. I concur totally with your assessment, and you did the right thing. And I say that without any selfish feeling on my part for wanting you back here. God bless you. Given the situation, Old Joe is the best we have, and I have confidence in my old friend. It might interest you that from this vantage point, the President asked my opinion when he decided to sack Bragg, and I wrote forcefully that he must choose Johnston in lieu of any others. He never replied, so I assume I displeased him as well," Lee said with a brief chuckle.

Longstreet grinned and noted, "Sir, I'm a good Corps Commander and I suppose the best the Confederacy has. I'm satisfied at this level. There is no time to experiment and see if I would be a decent Army Commander. I'm very glad to be back with you."

Lee nodded, smiled, and stood to stretch himself. "There is another year of battle coming. In fact it starts this week, May 5th if my intelligence is correct, with coordinated attacks all across the land. Grant is an unknown for me. I need your counsel on what to expect and anything you can tell me of the mettle of the man. I know you were friends in the old army, and he's married to one of your cousins. I've interviewed General Wilcox since he was also a friend of Grant's back in his West Point days. Cadmus says Grant's stubborn and focused."

Longstreet nodded and refilled his pipe and relit it. He stood and offered, "Grant has that simple mid-west temperament. Fell on very hard times and was living in poverty when the war came along. He is single-minded and unaffected by his losses to achieve an objective. Since he has material, supplies, and men in abundances, I think he will be relentless. We may lick him, but he'll just keep coming. All we can do is punish him so badly, the north starts howling. Lincoln will notice that."

Lee nodded thoughtfully.

"I'm surprised Meade didn't resign, but he's just a figurehead now. Too bad. I know the Meade type. I've been able to defeat or thwart every Commander of the Army of the Potomac. I'm sure what you say of Grant is true. Meade tried to test us a couple of times in your absence but really just half-heartedly, and we made no major mistakes. Still this army hasn't fought a large battle since Gettysburg, and it's time we got it back in this war. But those affairs about Mine Run exposed further flaws in my command structure."

Longstreet looked surprised but said nothing.

"Ewell was next to useless. He's married now to the widow Brown, and both she and General Early have him hemmed in and hen-pecked. If he doesn't show some of the ability he had before he lost the leg, then I will remove him. I really don't expect him to. I anticipate removing him within the month. As for Hill, he tried to take up the aggressive slack with Jackson dead and you gone. He made some terrible mistakes on impulse and lost several thousand veterans needlessly. I think he has learned, and he is a good tactical commander within known constraints. I plan to keep him if his health allows it."

Longstreet snorted and blurted, "You mean if the gentlemen's disease permits it!" The reproach on Lee's face instantly made him regret he had made the comment. Hill, as a cadet, had taken a fancy to a house of ill repute near West Point and contracted syphilis.

Lee put his hands on his hips, paced back and forth, and then stopped.

"We've six months to the November Federal election. We must not allow the enemy major victories, and maybe the voters will be so weary of the carnage in the fourth year of the war, they will vote Lincoln out, and we will have peace. That is what we will aim for. I know General Johnston shares this view as well.

This requires concentration of force. As it is, the President has Johnston's corps of Bishop Polk scattered all over Mississippi and Alabama and commencement of hostilities are at hand! There are at least 20,000 men scattered in the Carolinas that could be easily shifted here now. Not to mention six veteran brigades that properly belong to this army, including all of Picket's Division! Instead those men are idly down in southern Virginia and North Carolina.

I've tried time and again to educate the President that units are not abstractions on a map or on an order of a battle table. It takes time to get units accustomed to working together as larger entities like divisions. Instead he's wed to what he knows from being a Secretary of War back in the 1850s;

that means scattering men needlessly all over the landscape to placate governors and his own sense of geographical defense. Shameful!"

Longstreet was startled at this outburst of anger from Lee, who even now was red of face and panting lightly.

"Sir, sit down. I'm sure if you demand it or Grant starts moving his forces this week, then the President will have to face reality."

"Pete, all I've said is in complete confidence. You know that," Lee said quietly.

"Yes, of course, sir," Longstreet assured.

"The hour grows late. It will be dark soon. We should get down off the mountain and back to my camp where you'll be our guest tonight. Tomorrow we return with the other senior officers, and I will tell them what I think Grant will do down there in The Wilderness. Care to look through my field glasses or the signal folks' spyglass before we–"

"No, sir. Tomorrow will be here quick enough for that. Let's be off then."

Traveller took that as his cue and approached Lee from the side. Lee absently patted his flank, deep in his thoughts as he gazed out over the wilderness below.

THE BATTLE OF GETTYSBURG

If you have even the slightest interest in the Civil War, you must make the journey to see the sight of the War's most incredible three days of conflict. The best time, of course, is July 1st to July 3rd to see the re-enactment of the battles fought on this hallowed ground. You shall build memories that will last a lifetime and pass them on to others for years to come. I cried.

There are stories all over Washington that Lee is on the move and is in Pennsylvania with the Army of Northern Virginia. The War Department, and more particularly the office of General of the Army Winfield Scott, is a flurry of activity. Suddenly the word comes in that Lee is on his way to Gettysburg. J.E.B Stuart is in Maryland, and everyone has an opinion on where "Old Pete" may be with his huge body of men and material. The best bet is he is right behind Lee's advancing troops.

A clerk in Scott's office jumps up from his desk and looks at a map and says to a sergeant, "Where in the hell is Gettysburg?" Why would Lee take his army to that little town? The answer is very simple—multiple roads leading in and out of Gettysburg. Roads in those days were very narrow, and to move over 75,000 men and materials of war over one road would take forever, days, to arrive at the battle scene. The men would be strung out for miles and miles on both sides. Both armies needed several roads for this battle to take place on a timely basis.

Another factor was a sense of urgency for Lee and his men to attempt to end this war without further ado. The South was starving, his men were mostly without shoes, and a decent meal was only something to dream about. Many of the men had enlistments coming due soon and were bound to leave and head for home, and he had no way to replace them. His supplies for waging war were getting smaller and smaller.

The North had a new commanding general in Meade, and Bobby Lee thought he would be cautious his first time in a large engagement. What's that old saying "desperate times call for desperate measures?" The time to act was now.

THE TOWN OF GETTYSBURG

The population of Gettysburg at the time of the battle was about 2,400 people, including cats and puppies. The terrain is rolling, and the hills are somewhat wooded with farms nearby. There is a railhead in town and several small shops that are supported by the local population. A Lutheran Theological Seminary is in Gettysburg, and the setting is peaceful and serene.

I can't imagine what it would be like to be an expecting sixteen-year-old hanging out laundry on an early morning's hot summer day, having never visited another larger city, and seeing 150,000 soldiers a mile or so away getting into battle positions. The town's people must have been in shock at such a sight as this, realizing that their facilities both in terms of medical and physical building space would soon be overwhelmed. To further complicate or exacerbate the situation, on July Ist, 2nd, 3rd the temperature was almost 100 degrees and the humidity almost unbearable. The soldiers were wearing wool uniforms in all that sweltering heat, not to mention they had to fight in them.

THE BATTLE - DAY ONE

As mentioned before, the confederates needed shoes badly, and the rumor was that there was a shoe manufacturing company in Gettysburg. Of course the rumors were false and there were no shoes, but that was learned only after entering Gettysburg from the north and being repelled by Union troops.

Sometimes in battle situations, orders become confused, especially when bullets start flying back and forth. Such was the case for Lee's orders not to engage the enemy but to just locate them. He was entering the area blind; his eyes were the cavalry of J.E.B. Stuart, a.k.a Jeb Stuart, an expert at reconnaissance. Stuart was off somewhere in Maryland getting his name in the paper and too far away from Lee to be of value to him. With a disregard for Lee's orders, the two sides collided that first day.

The key to day one was General Buford because he arrived and positioned his men on the high ground and dismounted his cavalry to fight as foot soldiers. He was far outnumbered but sent a courier to General Reynolds to bring up his infantry to re-enforce his position as quickly as possible; he knew the key to the upcoming battle was strategic positioning of the Union troops under General Meade. Reynolds arrived in time to save the day and to solidify the best ground possible for the Battle of Gettysburg. Buford's men were able to start breathing again!

JOSHUA LAWRENCE CHAMBERLAIN

Any discussion of the second day of the Battle of Gettysburg must include a discussion regarding Colonel Chamberlain. Chamberlain, a school teacher from Maine, pulled off what would become a textbook maneuver at Little Round Top that other American commanders in future years would use very successfully. As we all know, he anchored the Union lines at the end of the fish hook covering the Union flank. If he fails to hold on, Gettysburg is lost, and General Lee presents the terms of surrender that he carries with him from President Davis to President Lincoln for signature.

Before the attack begins, Chamberlain makes his first of a series of outstanding decisions. He sends a company of troops down the hill on the right side with orders to take cover and wait to start firing when the battle becomes pitched. He orders another company to his left to act as a swinging gate down the hill on the left when he gives the command. The remaining part of his command will face the enemy at the top of the hill head on. His original force of 1,000 men in his regiment when the war started has been reduced to around 300 by the time he is assigned the flanking position, and his ammunition is limited.

When all looks to be lost with the Rebels swarming up the hill, not only does the gate swing at exactly the right time but Company B, which was thought lost in one of the earlier charges, rises up and starts firing into the advancing troops. Some Southern soldiers report after the battle that they were hit in three directions at the same time. The running comment was they did not care to ever see these troops from Maine again — ever! The Maine troops were out of ammunition at the end of the battle and guarded prisoners with empty rifles. Chamberlain saved the Union Army from disaster at Gettysburg, and the rest of his Civil War actions are available in bookstores and online.

THE AFTERMATH

In the Civil War, for every soldier who died in battle, two more died as a result of disease! Gettysburg was littered with dead men and dead horses. More Americans died at Gettysburg than in eight years of war in Vietnam. Houses were made into shelters for the wounded and dying, and everything in them was soaked with blood. Carpets, chairs, and various other things were thrown out into the street. The smell of death was everywhere you went and no manpower to help.

One doctor had ordered about 150 men he felt could be saved carried to a creek bank because there were trees and they would shade them from the intense heat. At the point of collapse, the doctors finished their work and got some sleep. That night a heavy rain fell, the creek rose, and the wounded that couldn't move, which was most of them, drowned! It took weeks to bury 51,000 men, not to mention thousands of animals, and somehow remove the smell.

Only one civilian was killed while ironing in her home, and that was a miracle. Today houses in Gettysburg still have mortar rounds stuck in their siding for one to view. There is one house that is said to be haunted by the ghosts of soldiers because of the extreme trauma that happened there. I guess believing this is an individual thing, but no one has been able to spend a night sleeping in that house since — no one.

The bell tolled for towns North and South. Clarksville, Tennessee had 960 men enlist in the Confederate Army. After Gettysburg only three were believed to have survived. Volunteers in a regiment from a university in Alabama after the battle had no soldiers left alive. A Minnesota Regiment took a terrible loss of life; 86 percent of the regiment was killed at Gettysburg, marking the worst total of any Northern force. Even considering Pickett's charge, the casualties on both sides were almost even. The North could easily replace their losses of men and material, but the South had nothing to replace with, and the result was that they would never again attempt to invade the North.

Robert E. Lee could not believe his good fortune. Meade had not followed up with an .attack to destroy his army. He led his men back to Virginia. The Confederate wagon train stretched out for seventeen miles, and Meade was fired by President Lincoln. The War would continue.

THE EARS GET EVEN LONGER

The saga of General Dan Sickles at Gettysburg continues, even after the conclusion of the war. Dan had a great idea, and he went to Washington to sell it to Congress to make the Gettysburg battlefield a national park resplendent with statues commemorating the bravery of units that engaged in battle there. Furthermore he suggested raising funds to have statues placed on the grounds of famous leaders who determined the outcome of the battle.

When you visit Gettysburg, you will find many statues of warriors, similar to very large trophies, of both sides and one large base with no figure on it. No cavalry rider, no leader with sword drawn, just a plain bronze base with the name General Daniel Sickles, etc.

It seems that Dan was named the treasurer of the group to raise money for the national park. Given Dan's proclivities to do the wrong thing at the right time, he managed to get caught stealing thousands of dollars from the donations for the National Park at Gettysburg! His punishment was no likeness of Dan will ever be placed upon that base or any other base in the park.

U. S. GRANT

In February 1864, Congress revived the rank of Lieutenant General, which until then had been held only by George Washington and Winfield Scott. On March 9th President Lincoln nominated Grant for that top rank. Then relieving General Halleck as General in Chief, he made Grant Supreme Commander of all Union forces. Grant assigned his command of the western armies to General Sherman.

Throughout the rest of the war, Grant was in constant communication with Lincoln either by personal conference or by telegraph. He was the first of Lincoln's Generals in Chief to have the president's full confidence. Lincoln had great respect for Grant's military knowledge, leadership, and strength of will, and he gave him wide authority for planning the conduct of the war.

Grant, in turn, set up an efficient command organization. He reported his plans and troop and supply requirements direct to Lincoln and Secretary of War Stanton. Grant's seventeen field commands, comprised of more than 500,000 men, were expertly directed with the help of General Hallek, who now served under Grant as Chief of Staff.

Now that he was in full command, Grant developed an overall strategy for the Union forces. Rather than capture cities or territory, he decided to go after the principal Southern armies. By coordinating the Union armies and the Union river fleet, he would apply relentless pressure against the Southern forces and wear them down. He relied on the economic strength of the North to keep him supplied with fresh equipment and troops while he kept the Southern armies from receiving resources of their own. Grant assigned the Army of the Potomac to engage the Confederate Army of Northern Virginia, commanded by General Robert W. Lee. Grant's western armies would meanwhile take on the Confederate Army of the West and sweep eastward through the South in a wide circling movement. Grant himself would accompany the Army of the Potomac, commanded by General George Gordon Meade.

THE WILDERNESS

Early in May, Grant led the Army of the Potomac across the Rapidan River in Virginia where, from May 5th to May 6th, he engaged Lee's army in the swampy, wooded sector known as The Wilderness. His losses there were appalling. For the next month, Grant's men fought in a series of battles against Lee's men, climaxing at Cold Harbor on June 3rd, where they suffered still more colossal casualties. On that day alone, Grant lost 7,000 men. His total losses for the month were nearly 60,000. As a result, he was called "Butcher Grant" by many people.

"I have always regretted," Grant confessed in his memoirs many years later, "that the assault at Cold Harbor was ever made. No advantage whatsoever was ever gained to compensate for the heavy loss we sustained."

After Cold Harbor, Lee took up a strongly entrenched position at Richmond, the capital of Virginia and of the Confederacy. Grant now altered his strategy. Instead of making a direct attack on Lee's well-defined position, he decided to proceed against Petersburg, the railroad and supply link to Richmond and the rest of the South. A great assault from June 15th to June 18th failed to take Petersburg, and Grant was forced to undertake siege operations.

PETERSBURG

From the middle of June 1864 to early April 1865, Grant besieged Petersburg. At the same time, he cut Lee's transportation lines and sent out flanking expeditions against the Southern forces. While Grant, month after month, slowly starved out Lee's men, his Generals carried out the other part of his strategy. General Thomas destroyed the Confederate Army of Tennessee at

Nashville. General Philip H. Sheridan devastated the Shenandoah Valley, and General Sherman marched through Georgia and South Carolina, destroying everything in his path that could be of use to the Confederate Army.

APPOMATTOX COURT HOUSE

By the end of March 1864, Sheridan had joined Grant in Virginia, and on March 29th, with an army of more than 100,000 under his immediate command, Grant began the final campaign against Lee. The end came on April 9th at the village of Appomattox Court House, Virginia. There, at Lee's request, Grant met with his defeated foe to discuss terms for the surrender. Because Lee was now Commander in Chief of all the Confederate armies, his surrender effectively ended the war.

Grant's surrender terms were generous. He allowed Lee's men to keep their horses and mules and he shared his army's rations with the Confederates. In his memoirs, Grant recalled that he felt no exultation on Lee's surrender. He felt "sad and depressed" and "like anything rather than rejoicing at the downfall of a foe who had fought so long and valiantly and had suffered so much for a cause."

Although Grant would later serve two terms as President of the United States, it was probably in the command of his country's army that his career found its true climax. He was a keen judge of military men and knew how to elicit their best efforts. If he was not a brilliant tactician, he did understand modern mass warfare. He could plan and carry out campaigns involving large armies and complex supporting operations. Personally Grant commanded the respect of his common soldiers, as well as his fellow officers.

A member of his staff, the younger Charles Francis Adams, described Grant's impact on his associates, "He handles those around him so quietly and well. He so evidently has the faculty of disposing of work and managing men. He is cool and quiet, almost stolid, and as if stupid, in danger and in a crisis, he is one against who all around...instinctively lean."

POLITICAL CAREER

The end of the war left Grant in charge of the U.S. Army, directly responsible to President Andrew Jackson (who had succeeded the assassinated Lincoln) and to Secretary of War Stanton but with ill-defined duties. In 1866 he was given the grade of full General, a rank held previously only by George Washington. He supervised the demobilization of the army and administration of the Reconstruction acts aimed at restoring the Southern states to full membership in the Union.

Because of Grant's great popularity as a war hero, both President Johnson and his rivals, the radical faction of the Republican Party, courted his favor. Although, as he admitted many years later, he "certainly never had either ambition or taste for political life," Grant was launched on a career in politics.

Like Johnson and Lincoln, Grant appeared to favor a moderate Reconstruction.

INTO THE HELL HOLE

The Confederate retreat after Cassville was punctuated by some discord and confusion. Corp Commanders Hood and Polk wanted to retreat to a better position. The solid professional Hardee bitterly protested. Johnston was reluctant to force the issue if two of the three corps commanders were against him, fearing word of discord filtering down through the ranks. Johnston reckoned he could carry Bishop-General Polk since he was really just a token figurehead anyhow in a corps where the division commanders carried the load of command. Hood was another matter. Johnston had ever growing good reasons to distrust the cripple.

This command structure of politicking and bickering in the senior ranks of the army was a bitter legacy of Jeff Davis who could have dealt with it in the past winter over the near officer revolt against Bragg. Even now a small fraction of Bragg die-hards, including Cavalry Corps Commander Joe Wheeler, were feeding information to Bragg in Richmond, designed to discredit Johnston.

Johnston, as usual, withdrew his army in good order south of the Etowah River to a strong position in the Allatoona Hills.

Sherman had no intention of assaulting Johnston's heavily fortified lines with the usual 1864 defense recipe of semi-clear-cut fields of fire, with stumps and debris left to break up any massed advancing columns. Topped off, of course, with chevaux-de-frise, i.e., frizzy horses the men called the forerunner of barbed wire obstacles.

Instead he re-grouped and shifted off to the west with most of his force aiming for a town called Dallas some fifteen miles south of the river and his railroad. That left flank of Johnston's was watched by the capable Red Jackson's cavalry division of western men brought over by Polk when his force arrived to reinforce Johnston at the outset of the campaign from Mississippi and Alabama. These were fighters after the Forrest mold, and Johnston pointedly had this unit operating independently and reporting directly to him and not Wheeler.

Jackson immediately detected the Federal movement. Johnston shifted Polk's and Hardee's corps over to counter. What followed were eight days of nasty, continuous engagements and battles. The Yankees found the going rough and hard where roads were scarce and water scarcer. Localized fights broke out over water sources.

Johnston got the better of it. Sherman lost over three men to Johnston's one as the Federals chalked up some 5,000 killed and hurt men over the course of a week.

This week-long campaign in miniature bloodied the ground about otherwise meaningless places, save for the few locals, such as Pickett's Mill, New Hope Church, and Little Pumpkin Vine Creek.

May 28th, Rebel cavalry detected a gap in the Federal lines isolating Howard Federal corps on Sherman's left. Johnston ordered Hood his right to seize the moment and assail the Yankees before the gap was closed. It should be recalled that a Federal corps was about the size of a large Confederate division, so Hood would have the weight of numbers. Nearing his objective, Hood claimed scouts reported the exposed flank was closed and the Federals' building earthworks. Without attempting to verify the sketchy information, Hood called off the attack, and another lost opportunity occurred.

Now in late May, it began to rain heavily. Sherman was stretched very thin, and his men were out or short of food since Sherman had only limited wagon transportation. Pondering all this, Sherman ordered his men back to the railroad. As he did so, Johnston ordered a series of savage little attacks while Sherman was in motion. As May passes into June, this round goes to Johnston.

Also at this time, Johnston learned from friends in Richmond that Hood was secretly sending messages to Bragg and Davis. Absent any paper proof,

Johnston could only limit Hood's role as much as possible since he did not have the authority to remove the scheming corps commander.

He did take the opportunity in May to learn more about his division commanders when occasion allowed. In the affair about Pickett's Mill on the 26th, Pat Cleburne's division had inflicted some 1,500 losses on the Federals at a small loss of thirty-five killed and 363 wounded. Intrigued by that in particular and the general's war long record in general, Johnston sought him out as Sherman recoiled his snaking columns in retrograde.

He reached him as Clebume was calmly surveying the Federal position with his field glasses. The constant of heavy skirmish fire crackling evidenced that Cleburne was harassing the Federal withdrawal. Johnston quietly rode up beside the rather thin man some called "the Stonewall Jackson of the west."

"General, how goes it?" Johnston asked.

Slightly startled Cleburne lowered his glasses and replied, "It's been a Hell Hole." He then smiled slightly.

"What?" Johnston replied.

"For the Yankees especially. That's what the men are calling this past week. We've given them hell, and Sherman's backing out of a hole! Thus the Hell Hole! That's what the boys are calling it." Both men laughed.

"Got to admire the men's sense of humor," offered the smiling Cleburne.

"I want to ask you. How do you do it? You consistently inflict larger losses on the enemy with fewer losses to your command than any division commander I know of in any of our armies."

"Oh, I don't know about that," reflected Cleburne with genuine modesty.

"I do. How do you work it?" pressed Johnston.

"Well I do unconventional things. All our regiments carry our special blue division flag, which the enemy recognizes. We do have a certain reputation."

"Psychology is a good weapon, and the Federals do know your men don't give up positions they choose to defend," Johnston reflected.

"As you know, I make massive use of skirmishers and have a large force of them specially trained and a special regiment of sharpshooters. They have a large number of those imported British sharpshooter rifles like the Whitworth model. All of those men are crack marksmen, and we train them hard and practice. If we are to advance, I keep my main force hidden but advance the regimental flags forward with them to give the appearance that they are the main body. The Federals volley, and my skirmishers work up to them Indian style, picking off the officers and sergeants. That goes on for a while. When we're close enough and the Federals are re-loading, the main force comes at a rush and try to run right over them, firing as we come," Cleburne offered.

Johnston nodded expectantly.

"On defense my skirmishers are serious about really slowing their advance on the same principal usually with the flags out with them, too. When we ascertain the weight and direction of the Yankee assault, the hidden main line is ready. Then they give covering fire as my sharpshooters run like the dickens into the main line. I always keep my men hidden and never standing on an exposed ridgeline or hill and so on. That confuses the enemy as to where my main line is," Cleburne expounded, warming to the task.

"Very effective indeed, General," Johnston replied.

"And I always try to attack in the flank or try to create one. I hate to make frontal assaults. They are a foolish waste of good men and irreplaceable veteran firepower," Cleburne said firmly with unwavering eyes.

"I agree, General. Give either side an hour to fortify, and it is an exercise in futility to advance with massed columns," Johnston nodded.

"Lastly I let the men know I care about them and detest wasting their lives needlessly. If I ask the men to do a hard thing, they will do it. I've earned their trust over the years."

"You certainly have," Johnston replied.

"You know, sir, when you took over and returned the regiments and brigades to the larger units they are accustomed to being with, that sure helped, too. Men like to kow and trust the men on their flanks," Cleburne mused.

Johnston nodded. Bragg had hastily busted up the armies alignment after the near mutiny against him in an effort to suppress loyalties. He lost Lookout Mountain largely because that was the last straw to the men in enduring him. After that they were indifferent to fighting for Bragg. Bragg lost his job.

"General Cleburne, there is a lot of hard fighting ahead. I need you. You know as well as I that after your circular last winter suggesting that we equip slave units and give them their freedom, it won you the undying enmity of President Davis and his administration. I don't think you'll ever make corps commander, although you earned that right long ago. I'm sorry," Johnston offered.

Then Johnston offered his hand. Cleburne shook it and made no comment.

"But now that I know this army and the senior officers better, I aim to use what resources I have to the fullest. That includes you. Expect to have large numbers of troops from other units temporarily attached to your command. I can't give you a deserved promotion, but I can give you more responsibility. You alright with that?" Johnston inquired.

Cleburne said nothing. A smile broke out on his face, and he nodded.

Johnston smiled, too. "Good day, General, and God go with you and your men." Johnston turned his horse and rode away.

AFTERMATH OF CASSVILLE

The argument had been going on for some time and gradually warming up as positions hardened and the niceties had evaporated.

"No, General Wheeler, you can't take your cavalry and ride around Sherman. We are outnumbered at least two to one. I need your cavalry fighting dismounted after patrolling on my right flank. There you stay. On the right. To the east, it is barren with few trails much less roads. Any flanking by Sherman's infantry, you'll easily detect in those thickets and pine barrens that stretch all the way back to Atlanta," Joe Johnston explained.

"But sir, we could cut the railroad and sever Sherman's logistics and communications. Then we could ride through Tennessee and into Kentucky and...by God right up to the banks of the Ohio River and scare the Yankees like hell," implored flamboyant Joe Wheeler with a hand sweep of his broad plumed hat.

Johnston sharply retorted to the surprise of his staff, "No, you won't and no, you can't. The days of joy riding and gallant chivalry by horsemen like you and Jeb Stuart did in 1862 and 1863 are gone. Finished! General Lee has Jeb Stuart on a tight tether, and I will keep you on one, too."

"Sir, how dare you insult me?" sputtered Wheeler.

"Listen to me. I know the track record. Your cavalry has never demonstrated any ability to damage Federal rail lines other than superficial scars. It's the same with Jeb Stuart. The only cavalry general we have uninterested in personal glory and determined to do the job is Nathan Bedford Forrest. His men don't carry swords, and they operate as mounted infantry as I'm making you do. When they attack a railroad, they bring heavy tools with them. They wreck the road beds, the culverts, the bridge approaches, all the dirty, grimy stuff you can't do galloping for glory," Johnston expounded.

Wheeler started to reply, and Johnston raised his right hand for silence. "I'm trying to get the government to release General Forrest and his command from northern Mississippi and onto Sherman's rail lines in Tennessee now. Between here and Chattanooga, Sherman has fortified the railroad with large guard detachments. He has a massive railroad construction force, too. That stretch is beyond our means. My policy is final. If you feel unwilling to follow orders fully, then tell me so now and I will relieve you."

"Yes, sir," came grudgingly and respectfully from Wheeler's quieter vocals.

He doesn't really understand. this war is no longer fun and adventure. It's life and death for the South, Johnston thought.

"Very well. You and your men have done and will continue to do very valuable service. I thank you. This meeting is dismissed. All of you may leave," Johnston said in the manner of a soft order.

Quickly the last of the officers and staff left the tent. It was after midnight. "Old Joe" sat alone at the table and gazed at the maps before him. It was much quieter in the camp now save for the occasional chirps of crickets and the low voices of some of the staff and couriers that worked the nightly hours.

Outwardly composed and serene but inwardly frustrated, General Johnston pondered the strange day's events that led to the foiled ambush about Cassville. Many officers, including the other two corps commanders, had expressed astonishment or worse thoughts concerning Hood's behavior to him.

At best Hood's explanation had been incomplete and failed to add up. How could the man that pushed for offensive measures at all costs timidly balk and fritter away an unmatched opportunity to punish a large Federal army?

Johnston thought back to his initial reaction on receiving word of Hood's behavior. Disbelief! How could a large Federal force be there on Hood's flank when Wheeler's cavalry had just swept across that sector to screen it? The subsequent excuse that a few very lost Federals were trashing about in the thickets was a pitiful excuse of a reason. Fifty thousand Rebel veterans poised to spring a superb trap on the strung out Federal marching column rendered useless due to 100 lost Yankees? What in God's name was Hood thinking?

Johnston shook his head in frustration and began to undress, removing his tunic. Easing over to his cot, he gingerly pulled off his long boots. Bending over he blew out the candle providing the dim illumination. As he did so, he reached a conclusion.

I cannot rely on Hood. At best he is unable to handle more than a division. At the very worst, he is not what he represents himself to be. Maybe losing a leg and an arm has taken part of his cognitive ability, too. General Polk is a great spiritual leader to the men but untrained in military ways as his vocation is Arch Bishop. I will use General Hardee for offensive opportunities and relegate Polk and especially Hood to static defensive roles. I will strip entire brigades and divisions from Hood and Polk to bolster Hardee, who is a good corps commander. And I will watch Hood's activities closely from now own. There is more about him than seems to meet the eye.

Satisfied with that decision, Johnston snatched up a thin blanket, threw it over himself as a coverlet, and fell into a few hours of deep sleep.

HOT DAY IN HARRISBURG

Hard on the heels of the triumph at Brice's Crossroads, Forrest faced fresh challenges. Major General A.J. Smith moved out of Memphis on June 26th with a veteran force of 14,000, including two divisions of the Sixteenth Corps. This excellent corps of Vicksburg campaigners had been slated for Sherman and the campaign for Atlanta but was side tracked by the ill-fated Red River Campaign of that spring. With this force, Smith was charged with the express purpose of keeping Forrest occupied and off Sherman's supply and communication lines.

On a personal note, Forrest was suffering badly from an attack of painful boils. Undeterred, however, Forrest followed a well-traveled path and began to concentrate his modest forces. Suddenly, on July 12th, Department Commander Lee ordered a change in plans to hasten a clash with Smith rather than follow the recipe of drawing the Federals further south and away from their supply bases.

The shift in strategy had as its catalyst fresh fears over the long-awaited Federal designs on Mobile, Alabama. In this election year, that vital open port city was the southern terminus of the area Forrest protected at the northern apex. In between was a food and granary growing region more vital than the Shenandoah Valley in Virginia and a vast infrastructure of war supportive industry. Closing Mobile to blockade-runners was one of the stated objectives of Grant's grand designs in 1864. As with Richmond and

Atlanta, Mobile must be held in this election year. With the solid defeat of Union General Banks' Red River campaign in Louisiana, credible sources in New Orleans got word to S.D. Lee that General Banks was preparing to set sail with a Mobile land assault force from that point.

Accordingly Lee had chosen a bold strategy of temporarily stripping the Mobile defenses to rush aid on loan to Forrest to turn back Smith and then return the Mobile garrison post haste. As it was, Mobile's defenses had already been badly weakened to bolster General Johnston's thin ranks facing Sherman in Georgia.

On the sultry evening of July 13th, S.D. Lee and Forrest conferred south of Tupelo, Mississippi. Lee had come with the troops by rail and met the cavalry commander in his tent.

"General Lee, I'm glad to see you," offered a smiling Forrest with an extended hand.

"You as well. I feel my bones have shaken loose from their underpinnings after that rickety train trip. I think our rails are about plumb wore out. Still the railroad men did their best with no notice to get the troops up from Mobile," responded a sweating Lee.

Forrest nodded and mopped his own brow with a kerchief. "If the Federals just keep on marching south in this weather, the heat will likely fell them by the hundreds and render the lot half useless," Forrest offered.

"If we had the luxury of time," Lee said as a wave of grimness shadowed across his handsome features.

"Major Anderson, point out the Federal positions on your map," Forrest directed his adjutant general as he spread the map before Lee on the small camp desk in the lantern light of early evening.

"Sirs, the position is a strong one. The Federals are encamped near Harrisburg, a small suburb of Tupelo near the railroad. Their infantry line is almost two miles in length facing west, with their left wing partly refused (drawn back) and facing south. They have Grierson's cavalry on both flanks. The enemy is improving their position with cotton bales, fence rails, and lumber from area houses they are tearing down, damn them."

"General Lee, sitting here is painful for my boils. Let's walk a bit outside and visit, shall we?" Forrest softly suggested.

"Certainly. Let's take a stroll and talk," agreed Lee.

Outside the tent, Lee led his superior to a nearby fire, motioning a handful of aides away.

"I would prefer not to fight here on the ground the Yankees chose," Forrest said firmly.

Lee nodded and said nothing, listening intently.

"Smith wants us to attack him. We learned over the past two years that frontal attacks on prepared positions manned by good troops are virtually futile for either side. It can't be our approach any longer. We can't squander our meager numbers so wastefully," Forrest opined.

"You are right. But we have no time, Nathan. We can't wait Smith out for a couple of weeks of slow Federal plodding across the countryside before he decides he's outran his supply line and turns back for Memphis. And his troops are top-notch veterans, too. I faced those men at Vicksburg last year. We don't want them in the Tombigbee Valley," Lee countered.

Forrest frowned and shook his head. "We must catch them on the move. That's where they always make a mistake, or we create one by playing on their fears with harassment of their flanks."

"Nathan, there is just no time. With the men I summoned from Mobile, we are about 9,000 strong here. I must take the Mobile garrison troops and some of yours besides before the Federals land their assault force to push on Mobile. Mobile must not fall," Lee explained with a resolute look to Forrest.

"Well 'course not," Forrest agreed.

"The Federal presidential election is just a few months off. So far the Federals have had no major successes and many defeats this year. The Northern populace is disheartened and war-weary. Just as Johnston can't lose Atlanta, I can't lose Mobile," Lee continued.

"We never have enough," Forrest expounded in soft frustration.

"What?" Lee said in surprise.

"Our constant juggling. Robbing Peter to pay Paul. Eventually one of those Federal generals will get lucky or grow some competence," Forrest mused.

"We have no alternative. We attack Smith and make those people scurry back to Memphis," Lee said with finality.

For a long moment, Forrest said nothing as he stared into the campfire light.

With a sigh, he replied, "Very well. I wish I could tell you it might work, but Smith's tough veterans aren't going to break from those fieldworks."

"Not likely. Nothing for it though. They can claim a mighty victory and retreat with honor at besting ole' Forrest!" Lee laughed sardonically. "Then we turn 'round most of the force to protect Mobile."

Forrest smiled, bemused.

"I might add that contrary to the persistent rumor, I'm not even remotely related to our great R.E. Lee, although I wish I had his skill. You know I served with him in the first part of the war up in Virginia," Lee noted.

"Well I'll give it my best and put my best face forward for the men," Forrest offered.

"I know…and so will I," added Lee.

The next morning, July 14th, the Confederate attempted an all-out assault. It was a scorching hot day with no breeze and total humidity. Advancing in those conditions was trying, even to well-conditioned men in sweaty wool uniforms. As almost always occurred in such hastily cobbled together ventures, units individually attacked with great spirit but in a most uncoordinated way. As promised Forrest offered no criticism of the plan to his subordinates and pursued it with his usual ferocious determination.

The butcher's bill included Confederate losses of 1,259 killed and forty-nine missing. Loss of senior commanders was severe in the cut-up regiments and brigades as they led by example. In Buford's division, every field grade officer was a casualty in one form or another. It was a tactical Federal victory.

However, the morning of the 15th, A.J. Smith placed his victorious force in retreat to Memphis, thus granting Lee and Forrest a strategic victory. To his victory at Harrisburg, Smith attached the highly creative excuse that much of his food supply had spoiled in the hot Mississippi summer heat.

Near sunset that day, Forrest suffered a painful foot wound as he led a pursuit to hurry Smith's retreat along. Smith was unaware of this as he continued his retreat. The wound, coupled with the boils, compelled Forrest to turn command over to General Chalmers. The Rebels went through the motions of harrying the Federals back to Memphis by the 17th. Forrest noted the Federal retreat was tight and well-ordered.

The Mobile garrison was returned to its home in time to learn that the danger from New Orleans was a false one for now. Oddly that battle would not be fought until R.E. Lee's retreat march to Appomattox the next year.

A.J. Smith telegraphed his bosses, "I bring back everything in good order and nothing lost. "

Again Sherman was disappointed by the inability of designated commanders to press on at Forrest. The South fought a fight it did not need to fight on that day and place nor in that manner. A.J. Smith's reputation was tarnished but not wrecked by his turn-around. Forrest was wounded and unnecessary Confederate casualties incurred. The affair at Harrisburg was unfulfilling to the gray and blue for different reasons.

RAID ON MEMPHIS

When General A.J. Smith returned to Memphis from Harrisburg, he quickly found himself under pressure of the highest sort from Grant and Sherman to produce or perish career-wise. With that in mind, he began feverish preparations to start out after Forrest again. The Atlanta campaign was mounting in intensity towards a climatic crescendo, and the top Federal brass wanted Forrest off Sherman's supply and communications lines, regardless of the cost or size of force needed.

With the heavy losses incurred at Harrisburg and exacerbated by the losses in the officer ranks, Forrest was in poor condition to counter another big Federal thrust. As the fighting for Atlanta raged, Smith prepared to move again in late July. This time his column would contain over 20,000 men in thirteen veteran infantry, three colored infantry, and four cavalry regiments. In addition the engineer battalions of the U.S. Military Railroad would come along to rebuild the Mississippi Central line as Smith advanced. There would be no going back for supplies as an easy out excuse.

Forrest continued to suffer from boils and the foot wound. Chalmers still remained in field command.

Meanwhile, President Davis had removed General Johnston as Army of Tennessee commander. Sherman was now at the gates, despite the skill Johnston has shown in retreating slowly, with his army still intact and morale high with an eye on the November elections. The impatient Davis ousted the army commander on the eve of the major fighting for the city. Davis had disliked Johnston since their West Point days. For a replacement, Davis chose John Bell Hood, he of the missing leg and arm. Hood was a good division commander in Lee's army with close supervision, but he was a head down sort of fighter with little strategic or even across the field tactical ability. He had often shown that as a mediocre corps commander under Johnston, and most particularly when Johnston had arranged for a giant ambush of Sherman's force earlier, only to have Hood blow the simplest of assigned tasks. Matters were made worse by Hood writing disparaging letters in reference of Johnston to Davis and his military "advisor," the despised former commander of the army, Braxton Bragg. Amid the hue and cry of the Davis action, the army's corps and division commanders asked the president to set aside the change for the duration of the campaign. Even the usually deferential R.E. Lee wrote Davis an unusually hard opinion that it was a mistake and that Hood was unfit for the job. Stung by all the criticism, the always thin-skinned and insecure President knew that it was too late.

So when Hood was elevated, his corps went to S.D. Lee, who was in turn replaced by Major General Dabney Maury as the department commander. Maury had been ably commanding at Mobile for some time, as was a West Point contemporary of Stonewall Jackson and George McClellan.

As Smith crawled slowly down the Mississippi Central towards Holly Springs, Forrest deduced the movement to be a massive feint. He telegraphed Maury that the real sustained move by Smith would be once again the Tombigbee Valley.

Faced with 4-1 odds and more so in firepower, Forrest, as usual, came up with a highly unorthodox solution. He summoned General Chalmers to explain it and his role as well.

Chalmers found Forrest sitting in a front porch rocker with extra cushions and his wounded foot propped up high on an empty cracker box. Despite the energy that always animated Forrest, Chalmers noticed he looked pale and had lost weight.

"I hope you are not in great pain. Is there anything I can do?" Chalmers asked with sincerity after dismounting.

"My greatest pain is the force Smith has got and what we can do about it. With that matter, you can be of good service," Forrest responded thoughtfully.

"Well the methodical way they're coming now and as tightly as they stay grouped, we can't do much more than remind them that we're in the neighborhood," Chalmers noted.

"Yep. That's why I'm splitting our force, James. You stay and put up a brave show to keep them occupied. Meanwhile, I slip 'round their right flank in this bad, awful wet weather and head for Memphis. We won't do much damage but," he paused, "it will put the scare in them, and soon Washington will demand Smith back track. Then maybe, just maybe, we can finally shake part of our force away and go after Sherman's supply lines as we've been trying to do all damned year," Forrest said with a sweep on an arm.

"Nathan, it won't work. This Smith is better than the others before him, and he has top of the line troops to work with. He won't fall for the ruse, and even if he does, we can't seriously occupy Memphis with that huge Yankee fort guarding it and the Federal navy on the Mississippi River."

"Work it well and you will help me. You may lose more men than we like, but I want hard, quick probing sorties all over Smith to mask our size and to suggest I'm still around. I'll be handpicking about 2,000 men to take out of Bell's and Neely's brigades. Only the most able with healthy horses and one artillery battery with double teamed horses will go. You bluff Smith awhile with the other 3,000 men and the artillery," Forrest coolly presented.

Chalmers started to protest again, and Forrest waved him to silence.

"Hear me out, James. You know how carefully I calculate these matters. We slip in and out of Memphis and raise holy hell while there. You know if we can capture some generals, so much the better. And I'm leading this in person, bad foot or not."

Grudgingly Chambers smiled and nodded. "Very well, I'll keep Smith busy while trying not to get crushed. He's got the force to do that and catch you coming back, you damn well know."

Smiling in turn, Forrest nodded. "I know, James, but they won't. I intend to plant false rumors of sightings of my boys all over west and middle Tennessee."

Thus in the drenching rain around the Oxford, Mississippi courthouse, Forrest handpicked his men and mounts. The men weren't told where they were going as Forrest's column steeled its way into the night, hidden by a rainy curtain.

Moving westward, then ahead northward, Forrest had to contend with swollen streams, paths, and roads almost impassable in the muddy conditions.

Improvisation was the order of the day. With characteristic ingenuity, Forrest converted his troopers into engineers. Grapevines prevalent in the region were chopped down and woven into suspension cables. Flatboats or rafts were placed as a center float or pontoon. Then bundles of poles were tied into the sides with vines to buoy the rafts, and finally, planks were laid across that were taken from nearby barns and gin houses. Horses could be taken over only a few at a time. Forage was crossed by an armful at a time. As always, when he was physically able, Forrest led by example. It was Forrest who grabbed the first armful of forage to cross the rickety bridge over the past flood stage swift moving Coldwater River, bad foot or not.

Moving day and night, the column continued its watery passage. Some 500 men or their mounts failed the endurance of it and were sent back. Eventually the men got the notion that they were headed for Memphis, and excitement permeated the ranks. Many of the men in the two brigades were from near there or actually hailed from the town. The forced march, hardship and all, began to assume a holiday air, and Forrest's officers had to constantly berate the men to keep quiet.

Finally, in the wee hours of Sunday, August 21st, the 1,500 wet troopers reached the city outskirts out of the 2,000 that started on the 18th in the Oxford public square. They were undetected.

Federal forces had held Memphis for over two years. So like Nashville, it had its large permanent garrison, massive fortifications, and swarming hordes feeding at the government trough. The town was swollen with government contractors, cotton speculators, settlers, and all manner of unsavory quick dollar types.

This day there were three Federal generals in residence. With Forrest's excellent intelligence network, he knew this and their anticipated whereabouts. District Commander Washburn and his predecessor Hurlbut were major generals, and Forrest assigned two of his brothers the task of capturing them.

Captain Bill Forrest and his band of scouts neatly captured the outermost picket points, but the next picket stations triggered a spasm of gunfire. Tossing orders aside, stealth gave way to excitement and "Rebel Yells" as the early morning riders burst onto the dark city streets. Bill Forrest was a younger, more compact version of his famous brother. His objective was to capture General Hurlbut, who was reported as staying at the famous Gayoso House Hotel.

"Come on, boys, the secret's out. Follow me!" he yelled to his scouts and he spurred his horse to a gallop.

Up the steps and through the wide and high hotel front doors, the mounted searchers burst into the ornate lobby on muddy horses, shaking the sleepy night clerk awake.

"Where's General Hurlbut's room?" demanded Captain Forrest as he pointed his Colt revolver at the clerk's head.

The shattered clerk hastily provided the desired information. The room was searched and found to be empty. In a surprise move, Hurlbut had spent the night elsewhere. Several other surprised Federal officers were not so lucky and were quickly captured.

Meanwhile, Lieutenant Colonel Jesse Forrest and his contingent made a beeline for the Williams residence occupied by General Washburn. In the nick of time, the sentry rousted the general who hustled out a window, absent his clothing, running into the night.

The sentry taken, Jesse Forrest burst into the bedroom to discover Washburn's boots, full uniform with accoutrements and…a pretty female companion.

Yelling to his men to hunt the General down, the colonel turned to the lady beneath the sheets. After polite but firm questioning, Jesse ascertained the lady was the wife of another Federal officer away with Smith in northern Mississippi.

"Well, ma'am, I can see no point taking you prisoner."

"Sir, you are a gentleman," the chastened lady demurred.

"Sometimes it's a weight, but yes, ma'am!" laughed the departing Forrest.

Poor District Commander Washburn made it safely to the protection of the seventy-seven big guns mounted at Federal Pickering aimed mostly towards the city.

Some serious Rebel effort went into looting government supply stores and capturing good horseflesh. But large chunks of the raiding force melted away for hours to be with wives, lovers, and family.

Federal reaction was disjointed, slow and feeble. The apparition of Forrest there was highly disconcerting. In this part of Federaldom, Forrest's reputation of doing the unexpected and succeeding was similar in stature to ROE Lee in Virginia. Of course Forrest knew that and used it as a weapon. General Forrest had absolutely no intention of taking the city proper. But human nature being what it is, Forrest let Federal fear feed all out of proportion on that notion. A more thoughtful, dispassionate, and analytical officer might have noticed that Forrest had "failed" to cut any telegraph lines that were frantically clicking outward for help in all directions.

By late morning, Forrest's main body was gone save for a few dozen laggards caught with wives or sweethearts and made prisoners.

Forrest took off south at a measured pace with large numbers of captured horses and about 600 half-naked captured soldiers. Losses were very slight on both sides.

An aggressive Federal Colonel Starr organized a hasty pursuit and overtook the Rebel rear guard a few miles south of town. The unfortunate Colonel Starr made the mistake of leading an impromptu, doomed out-molded saber charge. This brought the colonel eye to eye with General Forrest in a sword fight resulting in Starr being severely wounded by the general.

Earlier that year, Lincoln and Grant decided to end the parole exchange system that had worked so well and honorably for both sides as they chose to pursue total warfare. A generous Forrest sent a note offering to give the 600 prisoners back to Washburn anyway with a simple promise not to fight until exchanged. Both sides knew Federal prisoners were a hopeless burden for the strapped South.

Regretfully Washburn turned him down. But Washburn offered to send the men clothes, food, and a truce until the business was transacted. Forrest agreed, and the matter was concluded.

Forrest then returned Washburn's uniform and boots to him through the lines. In a chivalrous gesture growing infrequent by 1864, Washburn tracked down Forrest's own tailor in Memphis, his home town, and had a new Confederate uniform tailored to the general's measurements and sent over to him through the lines. On occasion it was still that kind of war.

Forrest's party returned home in much the way it had gone.

On one river re-crossing, Forrest scoured the evacuated banks for any picket stragglers. He found some.

"I thought I would catch some of you damn fools loafing back here in the cane as if nothing were going on," Forrest admonished. "If you don't want to get left here, you best come along with me."

The four cowed troopers hastily complied. The general stepped onto the raft boat, scarcely noticed. The Coldwater River was still at flood stage and would have to be poled across on the makeshift raft by this rearguard fragment with vigorous effort to offset the swift current. All lent a hand to pole and oar the raft over save one lone lieutenant standing in the bow of the raft. Forrest noticed.

"Lieutenant, why don't you take an oar or pole and lend a hand to get this boat across?"

Without turning to the voice, the young man replied rather arrogantly, "I'm an officer and I don't do such work when enlisted men are available."

The hard-poling Forrest responded by slapping the lieutenant hard across the face with his pole, sending the youngster into the raging river.

A rescue pole was offered the floundering young man. When he was safely aboard, Forrest yelled at him, "Now damn you, get a hold of the oars and go to work. If I knock you out of the boat again, I'll let you drown!" For the balance of the trip, the reprimanded officer made an excellent worker.

Recriminations and blame were quick in coming. Washburn roundly complained to Sherman and others that Forrest, with 5,000 cavalry, had given Smith the slip and not even been bothered on his return to Chalmers.

In fact Forrest had pulled the Federal panic levers just as he forecast. Smith had turned, but no Federal knew which Forrest sighting was credible. Indeed Chalmers pushed the retreating Smith so hard, he captured the intact Federal re-built Tallahatchie River Bridge above Abbeville and ninety-seven miles of telegraph wire!

From the Confederate perspective, the raid achieved the intended object of ending another Federal thrust at the Tombigbee Valley and the munitions-works at Selma, Alabama.

Sherman wistfully sent word to Forrest via Washburn that he "admired him for his dash but not his judgment." Washburn defensively labeled the raid as an "utter failure."

Federal General Hurlbut perhaps summed up the entire episode with his most enduring quote, "They removed me from command because I couldn't keep Forrest out of West Tennessee. And now Washburn can't keep him out of his own bedroom!"

THE ATLANTA CAMPAIGN

MAY-JULY 1864
Federal Army Commander-in-Chief Grant was determined to step off with a number of coordinated offensive thrusts threatening the vitals of the Confederacy the first week of May. The principal ones were those of Grant/Meade against Lee in Virginia and Sherman against Johnston in Georgia.

President Davis' policy of defense/offense was unprepared for these rather obvious moves by Grant. As a result, tens of thousands of troops were scattered in useless garrison work across the hinterland while Grant practiced mass and concentration. The result was needless crisis, loss of sustainability, and loss of opportunity for both Lee and Johnston.

It became obvious by mid-month that Grant and Sherman were conducting very different campaigns and would continue to do so. Grant was predisposed to maul and brawl right across Lee's lines regardless of casualties. Sherman detested frontal assaults and engaged in a chess game of flanking maneuvers with Johnston.

Eventually Sherman's larger force of 100,000 flanked Johnston's 60,000 out of a strong position about Dalton, Georgia near Chattanooga, Tennessee. While these operations occurred, the battles of the Wilderness and Spotsylvania occurred in Virginia.

Needlessly absent from Johnston were over 20,000 regular troops scattered in Mississippi, Alabama, Florida, and South Carolina that would arrive in driblets from the Davis administration over the next month. Had these men been present, Johnston may have been difficult to dislodge from the Dalton position with the force Sherman had at hand. Sherman could have swung over and around through Alabama, but that would have necessitated operations away from the railroad lifeline on which Sherman's force depended.

At no point, once operations commenced May 7th in Georgia, were there fewer than heavy skirmish casualties to the gray and blue antagonists in northern Georgia. In the mostly barren to hilly to mountainous countryside, neither Johnston nor Sherman could swing too far off the rail line between Chattanooga and Atlanta in flanking operations without great risk. Yet both did in an ongoing test of wits and intellect.

By May 13th, Johnston had taken up new positions about Resaca receiving reinforcements, especially what became Polk's Third Corps of his army from troops in Alabama and Georgia. Sherman continued his establishing pattern of limited probing on both flanks to test Johnston's strength, position, and probable intentions as a result of their locations.

On May 15th, Hood's reinforced corps advanced, sensing an opportunity occurring as Hooker's Federal corps also advanced. Hood was driven back, and battle level operations erupted along the line. Johnston's main position was judged too strong for direct attack by Sherman. Therefore Sherman got a cavalry and some infantry across the Oostenaula River south of Resaca.

That night Johnston withdrew his entire army and all its material intact across the Oostenaula River, burning the massive railroad bridge and headed south towards Calhoun and Adairsville.

On May 18th, President Davis telegraphed Johnston his displeasure over giving ground in northern Georgia. He sent no such message to General Lee in Virginia, who was grudgingly falling back, too.

Then on May 19th, General Johnston saw the moment he had dreamed of. The Federals had split to follow the two roads the Rebels appeared to have followed southward towards Kingston and Cassville. Johnston prepared a well-conceived classic "L" shaped ambush with Hardee's (left) corps and Polk's corps (center) providing the "L" and Hood's (right) corps situated to sweep in from the eastward side and potentially gobble up a third of Sherman's army and even the odds. The action was to unfold in a broad and open valley with Confederates on concealed wooded ridges.

The normally reserved Johnston felt good enough about the trap to issue an order of hope to his army.

Sherman had written Schofield, one of his principal subordinates, that he was puzzled about Johnston's intentions but determined to strike Johnston a blow before he escaped across the formidable Etowah River.

Sherman's host marched towards a trap unawares. Then General John Bell Hood shocked the entire Confederate host. About mid-morning, he sent word to Johnston that Federals menaced him in his rear in heavy force. A stunned and disbelieving Johnston replied that if it were so, Hood must drive them back.

The ambush ruined, the Federals made contact with Hardee and Polk and halted to fan out from column formation.

It turned out that the "heavy force" was a handful of lost Federal cavalry pickets wandering around in the thickets.

Hood had been secretly corresponding for some time to President Davis and his chief military advisor General Bragg that he wanted to fight, and Johnston wouldn't listen to his impassioned entireties to do so. He had also been fawning to charm Johnston of his loyal friendship. Hood realized that taking the heat over the spoiling of this unprecedented ambush opportunity might prove very difficult. Indeed whatever respect the Army of Tennessee had for his Virginia reputation was lost forever by this colossal inaction.

Hood immediately dispatched a Colonel Brewster to Davis and Bragg with a totally colored and untrue version of what had occurred since Dalton. This was unconscionable behavior both by Hood and Davis and Bragg outside the chain of command. Far worse was that Hood told Davis and Bragg what they wanted to hear, and they lapped it up.

With the passage of some 140 years, it appears quite likely that Hood wanted Johnston to fail. Hood wanted to be the army commander. The reasons appear on the surface like a plot in a cheap novel.

At Gettysburg thirty-two-year-old Hood lost an arm. Just three months later, he lost a leg in Chickamauga. That should have been enough to compel the retirement of any officer from active field command.

Recuperating in Richmond, Hood was vetted in the social scene. He took the well meaning flattery for his bravery for confirmation that he was more than he was. In blunt military terms, he was a great leader of the famous Texas Brigade, and Hood was a good division commander. But that was it. He was not a deep thinker and possessed only limited tactical skill. Both R.E. Lee and his corps commander Longstreet kept a tight control over his efforts.

Hood wanted to be in the favor of President Davis in Richmond the winter of 1863 to 1864. He angled for a corps command with the opportunity-laden Army of Tennessee. Both Lee and Longstreet weighed in that that was beyond his effective skill. Davis promoted Hood anyway.

As Hood made the social rounds, he also made an embarrassing courting fool of himself. Nobody had the heart to tell the wounded Hood to tone it down. If someone had, it might have altered the course of the war.

Hood attracted the cruel eye of one Sally Preston. She was a tease, a vamp, a collector of engagements, a broken heart inventor, and very bad news for John Bell Hood. The recovering hero began to pursue her affections. She played along, enjoying the notoriety and attention. Privately she told her friends she would never marry a cripple!

Soon enough Hood proposed. She stalled and enjoyed the chase. Eventually she told the hapless suitor that she would likely marry him if he became an army commander!

Through this period, Hood was in extreme pain and had become addicted to laudanum, a medical distillate of opium. Consequently Hood maintained a frantic correspondence with cruel Sally. To her it was just another lark. To the drugged-up Hood, it was a quest!

Note: Of course Hood's machinations will contribute to the removal of Johnston in July. He will then wreck the Army of Tennessee, lose Atlanta, and help mightily reelect Abe Lincoln.

THE HOWLING

On September 2nd, 1864, Washington received a telegram that Atlanta has fallen. Sherman is elated and wants all contraband destroyed quickly. Atlanta is the major railway in the South and a distribution hub. It's time for Sherman's neckties, the name given by his troops for railroad rails heated and wrapped around telegraph poles. His men, as expected, are burning everything in sight, leaving Atlanta in flames and exceeding his orders. Future plans for this fighting force are in Sherman's head and are at the least extraordinary. He said he would make Georgia howl and he sure as hell did it.

William Tecumseh Sherman was born in the state of Ohio and named after a Shawnee Indian chief. The name William was added after his father's death in 1829 by those who took him in to raise him. He was married to his step-sister and had eight children. He lived for quite some time in the South prior to the War and felt affection for the people. He was the president of a Christian academy. Once the War was declared, his love for the Union replaced all emotions within him for Southerners. In 1840 he graduated from West Point and served in the military for thirteen years. In addition he was a banker, lawyer, and a superintendent of a Louisiana Christian military academy. Louisiana left the Union in 1859, and he left Louisiana and went back up north, refusing a commission to serve in the Confederate Army.

In 1861 he was re-appointed as an officer in the Northern army and was promoted to Brigadier General and assigned to the Cumberland forces. His mental state became unstable, and he believed the press and all outsiders were spies and the War was to be a long and bloody affair that no one else thought possible. He became melancholy and returned to Ohio where he later considered suicide, and by his own account, only his children prevented this action from taking place. Next for Sherman was Shiloh, and as a Commander, he showed remarkable leadership and bravery having several horses shot out from underneath him. On May 1st, 1862, he became a Major General serving with Sam Grant at Vicksburg. He went with Grant following Vicksburg to old Tennessee and was promoted to Commander of all forces in Mississippi when Grant became the Commander of all Union forces leading the Army of the Potomac.

Following the taking of Atlanta and assuring Lincoln's re-election, it was time to act again. There was a meeting scheduled for 7:00 A.M. for all officers to meet in a large theater building in Atlanta to be followed by a meeting with all high-ranking noncommissioned officers. The men were called to attention, and up the stairs to the stage went Sherman, and the place went up for grabs with cheering and whistling from his cadre! Sherman, after several minutes, got them to be seated. They were told that they were going on an extended march with provisions for about sixty days and would forage for their needs as they moved. They would start at daybreak the next day and march to the sea! He asked if there were any questions, and hundreds of hands shot up.

"Commendable," he said and left the stage while his men roared with laughter. The meeting was over.

THE LOGISTICS

In 1992, at a location not to be named, my company sent computer network architects to guide several people through a process of recording every troop movement and all the logistics, down to the number of tubes of toothpaste our troops used until the fighting ended. The idea being if another engagement took place in the desert, we could supply a huge army with everything they could possibly need and a proven battle plan.

Sherman didn't come up with this idea or the preparation required while having a glass of wine over dinner. How do you march two columns of men

285 miles for 100 days and engage a force of unknown strength in the process? This was a well thought out process by Sherman and his cadre. The target was more than one city on the coast, it was the Carolinas, the very seat of the rebellion.

West Point prepared him well. He had acquired the best maps and engineering data he could possibly have for the march. His intelligence reports were excellent, and if the rains held off for a while, the terrain was good for the movement of troops. He had 8,000 beeves, over three million baked rations of bread, and various other items. All of that food would last a little over twenty days of marching. What about the other eighty days of the expedition? The order was given to forage for food and send large parties out to hunt, steal, and round up anything and everything that would allow his men to be fed. Burn anything in the process and destroy any salt mills or anything else of military value. There is enough ammunition and arms to carry on a minor war, and the erratic Hood was not in front of him due to poor positioning of his troops. At his disposal was every high-tech toy of the day, including the telegraph. Communication between the columns would be by runner, but location was not an issue–just look for the smoke in the sky because they would burn and destroy everything in their path. They had plenty of portable bridges to ford streams and in fact any wide river known to be in their path. How would he be supplied if he reached his destination only to discover everything he needed was destroyed in front of him? The reason to march to the sea — Yankee ships could easily re-supply him and his troops.

THE PLAN

The plan and the follow along objectives are simple in scope, but the execution of it will take an extraordinary effort with new approaches to war itself. Sherman believes the core plan is to defeat and erode the support that was very strong in the south. Let the impact of the war affect their daily lives and therefore limit their ability to support the continued conflict. As stated previously, his supplies were good for about twenty days, so his orders were to send foraging parties from both columns to take food stuffs from everyone in their path and then burn crops, buildings–anything that could support a war machine in the south. They were given the name "bummers" because of all the damage they wreaked upon the people in their line of march. Both of his columns would meet at the sea, and Savannah and Charleston would be taken. Sherman's orders were loose at best – take everything in the way of food but also make the south howl by burning and looting.

Another part of this plan was to free slaves at every opportunity further impeding the ability of the farmers to harvest their crops. It would not be the plan to take them with them because their numbers would only add to the burden of Sherman to feed them.

They were engaged to destroy any enemy forces they encountered during the march to the sea, large or small. Sherman's men knew he would not waste their lives, and unlike some other commanders in this conflict who wasted thousands, Sherman loved his men, and they loved him and called him Uncle Billy. Take Savannah, Georgia and make the South howl!

THE EXECUTION

On November 16th, Sherman's huge army set out to march to the sea and take Savannah. It is a miracle that only two rapes and a few murders were reported during this march. Many of these soldiers had lost friends and relatives in other battles and in other outfits across the country during this civil war. Even worse was the fact that these men saw their fellow soldiers who had escaped from Andersonville prison on several occasions during their march and foraging parties. Reports came in of men who were all but skeletons and had been mistreated beyond belief. If I were in command of Sherman 's army, there would not have been a prisoner taken for the remainder of the war. All prisoners, regardless of age, I would have had shot to death. Sherman's men let the dogs of war loose! Still, with all that said, after a large engagement with Rebel troops, to their horror they found the next morning their enemy was no more than young boys and old men. It was all the South had left to fight with for the rest of the campaign. There would be very little to stop him now.

Sherman himself may have had no love for coloreds as they freed them, over 25,000. He made it clear they were not welcome to come with him. Historians believe it was as much about how to feed them and they would slow his march down to a crawl. The upside to their coming with him was very little, but we will really never know what was in his heart and can only guess. Thousands were set free but to do what? No plan or provisions were made for this event or the ones to follow all over the south.

MERRY CHRISTMAS

On more than one occasion, President Lincoln told reporters and listeners that he knew what hole Sherman went into but not what hole he would come out of. A polite way of saying he had no idea in hell where Sherman's army was or if it was still in one piece or if Sherman was still alive.

On December 22nd, a message was presented to President Lincoln from General Sherman that said, "I beg to present to you, as a Christmas gift, the city of Savannah." After over $100 million in damage and a historical march to the sea, he had come out of his hole.

What has not been well chronicled is Lincoln's reply to Sherman.

My Dear General Sherman,

Many, many thanks for your Christmas gift — the capture of Savannah. When you were about to leave Atlanta for the Atlantic coast, I was <u>anxious</u>, if not fearful; but feeling that you were the better judge and remembering that "nothing risked, nothing gained," I did not interfere. Now the undertaking being a success, the honor is all yours ......A. Lincoln

Sherman said, "War is cruel and the crueler it is, the sooner it will end." War is and always will be hell.

SHERMAN'S ROAD SHOW
THE SHERMAN ROAD CONSTRUCTION COMPANY

All roads lead to Rome! They were the masters of road transportation and construction in the entire world until Sherman. The end of the war would now come soon for the march from Georgia north to pursue Johnston was in full gear. The roads his soldiers cut through and built through horrible terrain is a tribute to the physical condition of his army, as well as the engineering ability of his men. They covered ground on a daily basis that the Romans could have never accomplished in their best of days, in dense woods and swamps with heavy winter rains. The troops built twelve miles of road a day on average! The surrender of Johnston was to be next.

The war was over, but what was to follow was even more unbelievable!

JOE JOHNSTON TAKES COMMAND

The clamor had been ever too great for President Jefferson Davis to endure. The almost universally disliked Davis pet, Braxton Bragg, must go or there would simply be no Army of Tennessee.

With great distaste, Davis removed the man that managed to throw away the fruits of victory at Chickamauga some four months earlier and lose the "Battle of the Clouds" in a rout before besieged Chattanooga. To ease his own bruised ego and that of his discredited pet, Davis appointed Bragg as his Chief Military Advisor. The officers of the Army of Tennessee joked that was euphuism for chief mischief-maker. They had no doubt Bragg would use his new office for payback against his legion of enemies.

And with greater distaste, Davis reluctantly appointed Joe Johnston to command Bragg's old army. This shifted Johnston from his largely powerless position as central C.S.A. theater commander.

Johnston was fifty-six years of age and possessed a vigorous nature both mentally and physically from an adult lifetime of soldiering. His hair had become grayed and his hairline had also receded. Well-proportioned he was about 5'8" in height and slim of frame. He weighed not much over 150 pounds. Often he was described as intelligent, courteous, genial, and handsome with a rather unassuming dapper appearance. He invariably sported side-whiskers, with a moustache and tuft of a beard. Since his West Point days, one of his closest friends was fellow Virginian Robert E. Lee.

Johnston arrived from Mississippi at the northern Georgia town of Dalton on December 27th, 1864 via the state owned Western and Atlantic Railroad. That gloomy morning, he quietly assumed command of a dispirited force of about 42,000 veterans.

Johnston knew full well that he had his work cut out for him. His position hovered near Chattanooga and was largely sustainable solely via a single rail line winding up from Atlanta.

He quickly would find that the Davis administration expected him to advance offensively perhaps to the Ohio River. This with a spirit-broken army and solely lacking logistics to the extent of having no food reserves and not possessing a single pontoon bridge!

Johnston also learned that while in the spring, his army defending Atlanta would be one of the two key centers of Federal attention. Davis would not concentrate men with Johnston until the veritable last second. Vainly Johnston attempted to convince Davis that it took time to organize and mold scattered regiments and brigades into larger cohesive fighting units with group identities and their own individual espirit de corps that made the whole greater than a mere aggregate of the disparate parts.

Thus more than a third of what would become the spring Army of Tennessee was scattered from Mississippi to Florida to the Carolinas in small garrisons. This pleased local politicians but violated the basic military principal of concentration.

What Johnston could do was work on morale restoration and that he pursued as if it was a critical military campaign, which indeed it was.

Johnston had helped mold the raw, untrained human material as commander of what became the Army of Northern Virginia in 1862 when he was wounded in May of that year before Richmond.

Drawing on that experience, as well as his lifelong military experience, Johnston worked on repairing rank and file morale and healing the factions of the officer ship split into pro and anti-Bragg camps.

With his extensive logistics background as a permanent Federal Brigadier General and Quartermaster General of the pre-Civil War U.S. forces, he also undertook immediate measures to improve supply conditions for the cold shivering army.

Most of all, "Old Joe," as the men quickly came to affectionately call him, led by example. He quietly moved from camp to camp and campfire to campfire, he visited with the officers and men alike. Many times he was alone or had only an aide or two discreetly in tow.

The men wrote in their letters home and in their diaries and journals that Johnston was loved, admired, and respected by the men. Johnston returned the affection. He wrote to Davis that he had full confidence in the men's courage and fighting spirit, whatever the shortcomings in numbers and material.

A cold February evening found Johnston with his Chief of Staff, Brigadier General W.W. Mackall, completing a tour of Cleburne's division. The two former West Pointers were simply but neatly dressed in Confederate gray and walking through the camps of Brigadier General Hiram Granbury's Texas brigade. On these excursions, the two men usually brought with them some food to supplement the men's meager fare.

Johnston pointed and softly directed Mackall towards a campfire with about a dozen men. Rebel mess groups usually varied from a half dozen to twice that.

"Evening, boys," Johnston drawled removing his hat as he entered the circle of the flickering campfires illumination.

Seeing the three wreathed stars on Johnston's collar, the men came to attention in varying stages and saluted.

Johnston smiled and motioned them to continue on as he said, "I hope you don't mind, but my friend Mackall and I will be eating with you tonight. We brought some food we, ah, scavenged so we don't impose on you. Please share in what we brought you."

Mackall then produced in the firelight a haversack and handed it to a long-bearded Sergeant-Major. On inspection of the contents, the man broke into a huge grin.

"Lookee here, boys! Ole' Joe has brought us greens, onions, and a mess ah' tators!"

"I have a rather pitiful piece of hamrock as well," said Johnston, handing it over. "With these contents and whatever you may have, perhaps a Confederate stew is in order?"

"Right you are!" chorused several of the smiling men.

"If you men don't mind, I'll sit down a spell while your cook detail attends to matters. I fear my wounds of 1862 bother me a bit after a day of riding and walking about." Johnston sat on an old log.

"Yes, that's better!" intoned Johnston. "So what regiment is this, lads?"

"Sir, we belong to the 4th Texas Cavalry Dismounted. Sir, I don't suppose you're bringing us news that we're finally getting our horses back. I'm Sergeant-Major Raines," the man offered as he extended his hand to shake Johnston's.

"No, I can't give you that. I've heard the story-sorry that happened to y'all," Johnston said resolutely. Even a popular general spent much of the day saying no to requests.

Johnston was aware that Granbury's Texas brigade was composed of five cavalry regiments that had been tricked east across the Mississippi River with their horses left on the Louisiana side of the river in 1862 prior to the battle of Shiloh. The men's efforts to retrieve their mounts had all been in vain. The matter did not affect their fighting ability however. They were perhaps the best brigade in the toughest division in the entire Confederate army.

"Small consolation though it may be, boys, I can offer you some tobacco to augment your supply," offered Johnston handing over a large pouch tethered to his waistband.

"Bless you, General. We're not like the Carolina boys. Tobacco doesn't grow in Texas, and we're a long way from home anyway," Raines exclaimed as he passed the tobacco pouch around. Soon pipes lit up amongst the soldiers.

Pleasantries aside, Johnston and Mackall carefully and unobtrusively observed the men. They knew that Cleburne's division had saved Bragg's army from almost certain destruction at the battle of Lookout Mountain. If the spirit of this famous unit was torn beyond repair, then that portended a grim reflection on the entire army. Fortunately they saw the usual small talk and banter that signaled solid morale and self-confidence. Patiently, methodically, Johnston and Mackall asked the men individually about their families and personal situations. It was made clear that mail was a high priority to Johnston and asked the men to write or if they had written any letters they wanted sent by special courier across the Mississippi River for delivery to Texas. Mackall dipped into a shoulder bag and produced a sheaf of precious paper and some pencil stubs.

Johnston pretended to not hear the surprised whispers of the men proclaiming that the detested Bragg would never have done such a thing for them.

Johnston and Mackall then ate with the men and small talked of the simple things soldiers universally do when in the field.

"One thing, boys. In your letters, tell your friends and relatives that this army is never going to be flanked, surprised, or routed again. You've got my promise on it, and spread the word in your brigade," Johnston said resolutely as he rose to take his leave.

Looking about him one last time, Johnston knew he would have to use Cleburne's division in the hottest combat situations. He knew many of these men would fall this spring and summer, dead or wounded. Involuntarily he became misty eyed. Simultaneously the men reciprocated. They had soldiered since the spring of 1861, and this was the first time they felt they had an army commander that cared about them. As one they saluted as Johnston and Mackall left the light of the campfire and disappeared into the darkness.

"Sergeant-Major?" asked one tattered corporal.

"Yes?" replied Raines, half lost in thought.

"I think this army has finally got a commander that knows what he's about and gives a damn about us, too."

"Hell, Corporal. Let there be no doubt. The Yankees ain't gonna' fool Ole Joe one little bit," mused Raines.

Walking softly through the darkness, Johnston said quietly to Mackall, "I'm feeling very reassured with each of these forays of ours."

"How so, sir?" queried the chief of staff.

"The men just need some leadership, a purpose, and the sense they are cared for. These things I can give them–and hope."

"Sir, you're much too modest. This army's spirit was flat licked before your appointment. If you do nothing else in this war, it will rank as a noble achievement. Out of your earshot, the men and officers call it a miracle," opined Mackall.

"Well if divine providence lends a hand in this desperate enterprise we're engaged in, so much the better," offered Johnston, raising his hands upwards and ending the discussion.

UNCLE BILLY'S LUCKY SALVO

The rains that began in late May continued virtually each day through the month of June. In the aftermath of the "Hell Hole" adventure, Sherman's Federals had reassembled about their railroad lifeline. Sherman began to accumulate a supply store at Alatoona as he rested his weary men.

As usual Johnston shifted in response across Sherman's front. By June 4th his line was the strongest Sherman had yet encountered south of Dalton, resting on three large hills called Lost, Pine, and Brush Mountains.

Sherman pondered the latest Johnston obstacles placed before him and concluded that, since he outnumbered the Rebels two to one, he would stretch them out to the Rebel left. Then he would see if a weak point might develop in the lines about the three strong points.

Despite the muddy roads and inclimate weather, Sherman ordered a strong feint to his right to cause Johnston to extend his own thinner lines to see what might develop. In response Johnston prudently shifted Hood's corps leftward with orders to not bring on a general engagement. Johnston sensed a probable feint.

A couple of Federal regiments got lost in the underbrush tangle and stumbled into Hood's vanguard. The Federal reaction was to skedaddle back to their corps, which had already heavily fortified.

Hood's reaction was to dispatch his lead division in hot pursuit without bothering to reconnoiter, develop the enemy strength, or learn the terrain.

The result was that Hood's hapless, hard charging men broke out of the woods screaming the "Rebel Yell" into a cleared field of fire before the Federal entrenchments. In minutes over a thousand littered the ground. The Federals remarked they had never seen such an idiotic charge. Federal losses were a couple hundred. The whole position was designed to discourage any attack.

On receipt of the repulse news, the ordinarily reserved and placid Johnston lost his composure for an instant.

"Can the man do nothing basic right? General Mackinall, please send over word again that Hood is not to bring on general engagements. He is to probe with small forces and ascertain the Federal intentions only while serving as a defensive blocking force. Make that clear!" Johnston exclaimed in a raised voice.

"Better yet go over there as my Chief of Staff and deliver it in person. And take a couple of staff officers with you as witnesses."

"Right away, sir," replied Mackinall.

As the small knot of officers left, Johnston grew quiet and pensive. To himself he thought, is it his loss of limbs that enfeebles him? Is it his blinding ambition? How has his most elementary West Point training eluded him in his campaign? It is not my way to think so, but is this deliberate treachery?"

His mind made up, Johnston pointed to a staff major and said, "Ask General Hardee to visit me tonight. Just tell him we have much to discuss."

The major nodded, wondering what the remark might mean and half guessing.

Sherman was unable to detect any errors on Johnston's part, but the line extension did allow his larger force to creep closer to the Confederate lines. Then the Federal artillery with its component of heavier long-range weaponry could deploy plunging or enfilade fire on some portions of the Rebel line.

Concerned about the on-going viability of the line compelled Johnston to visit one endangered portion of Hardee's line on a spur of Pine Mountain on June 14th. He was accompanied by Corps Commanders Hardee and Polk.

The sight of three senior leaders of the army was a great curiosity to the men who began to gather in the hundreds despite admonishments from officers. Several colonels in the sector warned the Generals not to expose themselves as Federal artillery had the range and the position was under observation.

In the Confederate army, all officers up through the division level were expected to lead from the front and by example. But corps and army commanders, too, knew that word of their indifference to danger would sweep through the ranks like wildfire as a positive tonic to the men.

Ignoring the protests, the three generals climbed to the escarpment above the breastworks and peered out for a view with their field glasses.

By sheerest chance, Sherman was opposite and below them staring up at the Confederate lines along the skyline. He noticed several hundred Rebs were mingling about and staring in the same direction. He saw the object was three officers scanning the Federal position.

Also, by pure chance, a crack sniper of Cleburne's elite sharpshooter regiment was scanning the vicinity from more than a mile away in a shadowy hollow beneath a rotted log. Using the modern high-powered telescope fitted to his futuristic high-powered imported British Whitworth rifle, he spied Sherman and his party. His telescopic lens was far more powerful than the standard field glasses.

The sniper, actually an ordnance sergeant named Oscar Holliman, hailed from Arkansas.

Oscar was detailed to this special unit from Galvan's stout Arkansas brigade of Cleburne's division. A gunsmith by trade, he was thought to be perhaps the best shooter (the term of the time) in the entire division.

Oscar was both literate and reasonably well-informed. Pictures were circulated amongst the special men such as him, and he thought he had a good fix on none other than William Tecumseh Sherman or Old Billy sitting on a horse.

Carefully weighing the distance of a mile and the wind and problem of shooting steeply downhill, Oscar made his adjustments. Cradling his expensive rifle ($1,500 gold in 1864 or about a million in 2005 paper dollars), he exercised breath control and calmly squeezed the trigger. It was an extreme long shot by any measure.

Sherman was below the zone of hearing from the rifle's report. He did hear a familiar bullet "whoosh" whistle down, and his horse whinnied as it shifted to its right.

Irritated now he dropped his glasses and noticed a six-gun battery of long-range Parrott cannons in hailing range.

"You boys! Give them a few salvos up there where they've bunched to-gether. Shoo that clump of officers off and make them scatter," Sherman yelled.

Replies of glee for "Uncle Billy," as his men called him, came as the men swung into action.

Oscar observed he had failed to hit Sherman and concluded the extreme range too long and too problematic that far downhill. He turned to nearer targets of opportunity.

Generals Johnston, Hardee, and Polk were engaged in an absorbing con-versation. Besides the topic of holding the current line, the senior officers had visited the problem of what to do about Hood. Pulling back the line had been concluded, but what to do about Hood other than restrict his potential damage had not been discussed yet when the sounds of canon fire interrupted the meeting. Hood was mentally imbalanced due to losing an arm and a leg in the war in different engagements. His decision making became very poor, and they wanted no more of his poor judgment when leading thousands of men in battle.

The concussion of the battery salvo off the hill was heard by the generals since they were above it, but they did not notice the puffs of smoke from their left and below. Almost immediately the gathered Rebel throng, men and officers alike, shouted in one variant or another "Get down, run for it, watch out," and the like.

West Point trained engineer Johnston was a master at usages of the con-tour of the land. His standard entrenchments provided for trenches perpen-dicular to the lines facing the enemy or what were called revetments then, and bomb proofs in later wars. Johnston and Hardee took off for them as did the dispersing host. Bishop-General Polk did not.

Leonidias Polk was a one of a kind original in the war. The Arch Bishop of the Episcopal Church in the Southern States, he was also a West Pointer and friend of Jeff Davis. He was not an astute military man and made no claim to be. While unsuited to be a proper corps commander, he was the moral authority of the Army of Tennessee. Polk was the "Marse Robert" that Lee was to the Army of Northern Virginia. It was Polk that glued the morale of the army together through the years of sorry leadership from first Albert Sidney Johnston and then Braxton Bragg, and for some of the men,

John Pemberton. All Davis' pets. It was Polk that led the religious revival that sustained the army after the debacle before Chattanooga in the winter of 1863. He was worth 10,000 men.

Polk, like most of his faith in that time, lived by a certain fatalistic stoicism regarding life. In soldier terms, if your time was up, then it was up. Like Lee, J.E.B. Stuart, Jackson, and a host of other Episcopalians, he placed his fate in God's hands in this manner. He was also aware that as a man of God, he could never show caution or fear as an arch bishop. His corps commander role lost out in this internal duel of wills, even though a chorus of voices yelled for Polk to get down.

The Federal artillery battery commander had selected bolt shot to do the dispersing. These were iron pieces shaped somewhat like modern hand weights with perpendicular ends. One fired per gun. The in-flight effect was to cause them to fall end over end. They were very effective long-range ordnance at bowling through multiple ranks of soldiers massed in columns as they could sheer through and dismember man after man and cause panic.

As the first salvo struck home, most of the Rebels had found cover, including Johnston and Hardee. Polk was still walking along, despite entreaties to hurry up. Then, as the second salvo howled in, something on the ground caught Polk's attention. He stopped with his back to the Federal fire.

The second salvo screeched into the Confederate lines. One of the bolts whizzed end over end in a blur and ploughed straight through General Polk's back and out the front, taking most of his torso with it some distance beyond.

Cries of dismay erupted from the Confederates. General Polk was a big, broad shouldered man, some six and a half feet tall. It was not clear he was dead as mercifully none had seen the gory moment of carnage. As many rushed to his aide, the third round came in.

A scuffle erupted when Army Commander Johnston attempted to go to Polk's aid. A dozen officers and men knocked him to the ground and covered him with their own bodies until the third and final salvo subsided.

"Let me up, damn it. Let me up!" demanded Johnston. He was helped to his feet and pushed past the others to the remains of Polk.

Absently Johnston brushed his grayish hair with his dirty fingers. He noticed a bulge in one of the General's pockets. He fished in a hand and retrieved four pocket testaments, the little bibles Southern fighting men carried. The testaments were covered with blood. Wiping the blood away with his uniform, he opened the front page of the first and noticed it was inscribed to him with a personal message. The next, dedicated to Hardee, and so on. He stuffed them in his own pocket. He stood and began to weep.

All about him he observed men crying as well. The army had seemingly lost its conscience. With tears streaming down his face, Johnston summoned his voice in a slightly wavering tone.

"Listen to me, boys. Listen to me. He is with the Lord now. He is looking down on us right now. We must continue the fight. What else can we do? He would want you to. If the Yankees want to destroy us, have we any other choice? Resolve to fight on as he would tell you!"

Johnston drew his sword from its scabbard and raised it above his head. Slowly he gazed at the men and turned about him in a circle. It grew quiet. Then Johnston just stood there, sword held high. Other officers drew their swords and raised them up in salute. Soldiers raised their rifles.

Someone let go with the defiant enraged version of the "Rebel Yell." Like a spark on a kerosene fire, the cry was taken up by the host. Over and over the ragged veterans screamed it. It echoed across the hills as other Confederate units took it up. Federals listened in awe.

The Army of Tennessee was not done yet.

The next day, Federals captured a few Rebel pickets and learned that Polk had died on Pine Mountain. Further the rumor was that Sherman had called the shot and taken deliberate aim at an Episcopal Arch-Bishop. More so the Confederate troops were in a vengeful spirit and would remember.

While not especially religious himself, Sherman had no desire to ignite a religious crusade against him. He quickly sent word over that the rumor was false and expressed his regrets over Polk's death.

Polk was the highest religious figure killed in the war. The only other Confederate officers of like or higher military rank to be killed were Albert Sidney Johnston and Stonewall Jackson.

Ahead lay Kennesaw Mountain.

SURRENDER OF THE ARMY OF NORTHERN VIRGINIA

AND THE BEGINNING OF A MIRACLE OF WAR APRIL 9th, 1865

After years of war and countless wounded and dead, on April 9th, 1865, the American Civil War ended. It ended in Wilbur McClain's home in his parlor, and that was fitting since it started with a shell in his summer kitchen at the first battle of Bull Run at the outset of the war. He moved his family out of harm's way to a small community called Appomattox Court House in Georgia. Never did he imagine this war would end in his home in his parlor with the finest leaders on both sides sitting at his table.

It was a cool morning, and General Lee came over to the area where Traveller had been posted. He played with his ears and said good morning to his favorite horse in the world. He had attempted one last breakout from the oncoming Union host. His officers in the field reported that, upon reaching the top of a good lookout point, that all they could see to the horizon was a sea of Union blue.

For two days couriers had delivered messages back and forth to the Army of the Potomac regarding a cessation to the fighting. Both Lee and Grant felt that further bloodshed was inappropriate since the South could no longer be considered an enemy of strength.

Robert E. Lee and Ulysses Simpson Grant had met before the meeting, ending the Civil War. Both men had served in the war against Mexico–Lee with great distinction and Grant as an up and coming officer. They had both been professional soldiers in the service of the American Army. They had both graduated from West Point as part of the long gray line. Today they would make history, and "The Miracle of War" would have its seeds planted.

A MAN CALLED SAM

Ulysses Simpson Grant was another man from Illinois whose contribution to the Civil War and its outcome and its aftermath are far reaching. Today he will accept the surrender of the Army of Northern Virginia, General Robert E. Lee commanding.

Sam Grant was a clerk in a clothing store in Galena, Illinois and had failed in every business venture in which he had ever been involved. His only real success was in his marriage and his military service in the Mexican War. He had graduated from the military academy at West Point with the worst grade point average in his class. Rumors had it that alcohol dominated his life and that he had long periods of depression.

The Civil War started, and he could not wait to be back in uniform again. The Mexican War had given him a good reputation as an officer who remained cool under extreme pressure and driven in his beliefs on how the conduct of a battle should be concluded. Sam asked for no quarter and gave no quarter when engaging his foes. He led his men on two campaigns capturing Forts Henry and Donaldson and in both cases, demanding immediate and unconditional surrender. The South now understood what his initials "U.S." really meant, and so the nickname for him was "Unconditional Surrender Grant."

The first huge battle of the war took place near Corinth, Mississippi near the Tennessee border. He and General William Tecumseh Sherman were given the task of capturing and destroying the railhead and shipping facilities at Corinth. However, with all the planning in the world, things have a way of changing. In the morning mist at a place called Shiloh, the armies ran into each other by accident, and the battle was on. Shiloh is a Hebrew word meaning "place of peace." For many who fought there, it meant "rest in peace." Many books have been written about this battle, and for me to go into detail about it would only be redundant. However, there is a telltale trait that emerges in Grant, and it is worth discussing in this book. Grant's coolness under fire is uncanny, and after the first day's battle with heavy Union losses, Sherman told Grant that "we have had the devil's own today."

Grant's reply was, "Yeah, but we will whip them tomorrow." A shocked Sherman stood there in silence. On the second day, a Union victory was completed with massive casualties on both sides. Grant was fired from his post, undefeated as a general. One thing few historians seem to touch on was that Grant understood the superiority of numbers. My dad once told a friend who was about to bring suit against the Internal Revenue Service that "when taking that kind of action, one should count soldiers, and they have one hell of lot more soldiers than you do." Later in the war, Grant's understanding of his numerical superiority would serve him and the Union well.

After the war, Grant had throat cancer and was financially ruined. He wrote his memoirs of the Civil War with the assistance of Mark Twain, and shortly afterwards, he died. His memoirs were published, and his family's fortune was once again restored. That set the stage for the government to enact legislation granting a pension to former Presidents of the United States. Never again would a former President leave office and become penniless.

Not too many years ago, Grant's tomb was again broken into in New York and battle flags and other items stolen. It is the most visited sight in New York and the city of Galena, Illinois, and the state of Illinois demanded their hero be protected or return him to Illinois where protection would be assured…hang your head, New York!

THE FINAL MESSAGE

After several communications back and forth, Lee agrees in principle to the terms of surrender. A meeting time is set for April 9th in Wilbur McClain's home with the parlor as the room of choice for the formal ceremonies.

Robert E. Lee arranges to have his best dress uniform laid out, along with his engraved dress side arms and sword. He looks like an aristocrat, and his posture for a man of his age is remarkable. An officer's call is held in his field headquarters, and his men are told that he would attempt to arrange for the best possible terms.

As he leaves his headquarters and walks over to his aid, he notices Traveller has backed up a few paces after seeing him. Traveller's head lifts and shakes as if to say I am up for the occasion! The ride in is quiet, and the reality of it all begins to sink in his mind, and the thousands of details of things that must be done surface rapidly. The war has been long with hundreds of thousands of casualties, and in a short while, all of that will be set aside.

General Lee arrives first and looks relaxed yet very alert. General Grant arrives from the field in a plain uniform that is dusty and somewhat dirty. His rank is not apparent, and he apologizes to Lee for his appearance. Plain dress is nothing new to Grant. When President Lincoln promoted Grant to the rank of Lieutenant General, he summoned Grant to a reception that was to be held at the White House. Upon arrival in Washington, Grant and his son checked into Hull House and asked the clerk for a room. He was told the place was packed and the only room available was some five floors up without a view, and that was acceptable to Grant. The clerk instructed him to sign the guest registration book, and upon signing it, he turned back in front of the clerk for viewing. The clerk could not believe his eyes and that the man in the plain dusty coat was the new Four-Star General commanding the Army of the Potomac!

Grant tells Lee he remembers meeting him before, but Lee doesn't remember Grant. Their conversation is very friendly, and after a period of time passes, Lee reminds Grant as to why they are having this meeting. An American Indian of the Seneca Nation is to memorialize the surrender in writing. Lee offers Grant his sword and his sidearm in a customary fashion, and Grant tells Lee to keep them. As the terms of the surrender are dictated to the clerk, the clerk suddenly stops and breaks into tears. He cannot continue and leaves the room.

Both men sign the document ending the war, and Grant asks Lee if he has any special needs for him and his men. Lee can't quite remember when last his men ate a real meal, and Grant asks how many men are left in Lee's command. Lee isn't sure but estimates around 18,000 men. Grant orders an officer to have delivered 25,000 rations for Lee's army. At a later date, Grant will ask Lee to encourage all Southern leaders to bring about a peaceful surrender. Lee states that General Johnston will bring in his command and stack arms as soon as is practical.

The men shake hands and depart, and the foundation for a "Miracle of War" is put in place.

A MIRACLE OF WAR - FINAL CHAPTER

It doesn't seem possible, but the killing stopped, no gorilla activities in the hills, no companies of men engaging in battle. The South had been welcomed back into the Union, and numerous southern senators and congressmen returned to their jobs in Washington. For the first time, people talked about these United States of America. As soldiers men had traveled in many states where before most lived and died and spent their lives within twenty miles of their place of birth. We weren't just states but a country for the first time in our history.

Thousands of plates used in photos of the war were placed in greenhouse roofs. It was as though no one could conceive that the war ever occurred or could have ever occurred.

Today we are appalled at the number of deaths in civil wars in other countries when they approach 50,000. How dare we. We lost 600,000 in our Civil War, over 2 percent of the entire population of Americans.

The war ended, really ended, unlike Bosnia and a thousand other civil wars in history. There is a movement out there to re-write our history; I can think of no greater dishonor to these men who gave the last full measure.

God bless America.

RATING THE GENERALS OF THE SOUTH 1861-1865

(A Subjective Opinion)

This book largely deals with the final eighteen months of the Great War we call our Civil War. It cost over a million deaths and badly wounded. No one would have sought such a war, except for a few rabid abolitionists in the North and a handful of large planters in the South. These losses were out of a population of some 3.5 million by the 1860 census. The analogy would be some 6 million in such losses in our present population terms. Frankly hardly any of those killed and hurt gave a hoot about slavery, the union, states' rights, tariffs, perceived slights, and the like. Mainly they behaved as they did to not let their friends and comrades down on the field of battle.

Great wars take on a brushfire life. Once the beast is unleashed, it is seemingly impossible for politicians to turn off the bloodletting.

The South could never win by victory if you define it by destroying the other side's great armies in a few great battles. Firepower had advanced by this time to inflict great loss, but logistics had not kept stride.

It all came down to staying power. The year 1864 was a Federal election year, and the unpopular Lincoln was up for re-election. He needed to have great symbolic victories to show massive progress. The South could not win but perhaps could gain a negotiated peace and retain nationhood by not losing. This essay is about many of the major players in that struggle on the Confederate side. The South came very close to pulling it off. The flaws noted below by some major players changed the future of our United States.

On one level, it is very unfair to play armchair quarterback with history, but all aficionados of history tend to do it. True, the participants were caught up in the immediacy of the moment, usually under pressure and with much less information and facts than the present-day reader. On the other hand, if you study the era as I have for some forty-four years, you will form a body of opinions.

Below I rate the major Confederate players concerned with the period encompassed by the book. As a caveat, I agree with the late Shelby Foote. Shelby said that he didn't think any of the bunch was cowardly, deliberately set out to do poorly or make bad decisions, and none had traitorous designs. So before I judge, let me say across the board that I think they gave it their best, even if the best for too many of them just wasn't good enough for the situation at hand.

I use an old-fashioned scale of A to F. The ratings are skewed heavily toward the 1864-65 era. However, if the individual continues to commit the same blunders of the 1861 to 1863 periods, they aren't learning and growing, and that influences my tally.

This scoring will likely appear in the book in some form as an appendix. Or this may be reworded as part of the introduction, similar to what Douglas Southall Freeman did in his Pulitzer Prize winning *Lee 's Lieutenants*.

In any case, for those of you that haven't had the time or inclination to read all the draft chapters, this serves as a guide to the major players in the book.

PRESIDENT JEFFERSON DAVIS — D

This Mississippi Senator was not one of the "fire-eater" hotheads that propelled the South into secession. He did not campaign or desire the Confederate presidency. Sadly he saw himself as possessing a great military mind. This view was based on attending West Point, a brief lark commanding a militia regiment in the Mexican American War and a stint as U.S. Secretary of War in the 1850s. His pre-occupation with clerk level military details caused him to woefully neglect Confederate economic, monetary, and foreign policy. His personality was such that he failed to cultivate the goodwill of the powerful state governors.

He had little skill in choosing commanders and administrative leaders. This trait was disastrous in 1864-65. It would be unrealistic to expect him to select wise choices for military or government positions of prominence without some blunders. Lincoln made plenty of dud choices, too. The difference was that Lincoln tended to toss the unworthy to the side fairly quickly. Davis absorbed criticism of his dumb bunnies by internalizing it. The thin-skinned Davis would "stand by his man," no matter how costly to the Confederacy. Because he was familiar with a peacetime army dispersed into departments and districts, that's how he set up the Confederate military. This violated the axiom of concentration of mass necessary in wartime. It also encouraged local commanders to run their own little fiefdoms with little or no mutual cooperation.

To his vast credit, he avoided many of the civil rights abuses Lincoln imposed on the North. He didn't jail citizens that criticized him, suspend the writ of habeas corpus carte blanche (i.e. you can't be jailed without formal charges and a court date set), shut down critical newspapers and smash their printing presses, and imprison state legislators and politicians for opposing him. He also didn't send soldiers to arrest citizens at the point of bayonets. Lincoln imposed all these outrages and held some 20,000 hapless Northerners through the war without a trial.

Davis was very intelligent but not a particularly creative thinker or a quick responder to crisis. As the president, he should have squashed the early blunder to move the capital from the protected central South to Richmond, a mere 100 miles from Washington. While this move was done mainly for the comfort of the politicians who felt cramped in smaller Montgomery, that is no excuse. At the very least, he should have insisted the administrative capital remain safe deep in the interior while the legislative capital would vary its location. This would have avoided the "saving face" trap that had Lee's army glued to Richmond through its entire existence.

Although Davis was quite willing to free blacks that fought, he stalled until February 1865 when it was too late. He also stalled on proposing a gradual emancipation, although he was open to it. He should have at least openly acknowledged and praised the tens of thousands of free blacks and servants that were voluntarily serving in the ranks to steal some of Lincoln's artificial and sanctimonious cleverness. When Lincoln and Grant cruelly and coldly ended the very successful and humane prisoner of war exchange program in early 1864, Davis blew a big chance to hurt Lincoln's re-election prospects. Davis could have simply released the Federal prisoners under parole to go home and marched them towards the Federal lines. The South really couldn't afford to feed them anyway, which is what Lincoln and Grant were trying to exploit regardless of the human cost. If Davis had released the men, Lincoln would have looked very inhumane in the eyes of northern voters by comparison to the statesman-like Davis.

The 1850s-60s was not a time of strong leadership in the nation. This is largely why we plunged into a bloody civil war nobody really wanted. Still, once drafted into the presidency, Davis gave it everything he had. The forging of a nation under a massive military attack by modern weapons unprecedented in human history was a daunting task for any man. In the last months, he exhorted the citizenry to practice guerilla warfare and continue the struggle forever. Wisely the generals and the soldiers ignored him as generals sagely arranged their own individual unit surrenders. By late 1864, he had clearly lost his grip on reality and fell into a form of dementia. Davis had impeccable devotion, resolve, and integrity. It was not enough.

GENERAL BRAXTON BRAGG — F

It is hard to find anything attractive to say about this man. He came into the war the same mean, crabby, and self-serving cretin he had always been. Years earlier Bragg had been assigned two jobs at one of the army's many small frontier posts. Bragg was a stickler for regulations. He found his task required that he place himself under arrest since his multiple jobs required he take differencing positions.

When he explained this dilemma to the post commander, he is said to have exclaimed, "Dear God, Mr. Bragg, you've argued with every man in the army and now you're arguing with yourself!"

Only Davis ignored the universally held view that Bragg was a failure as commander of the hapless Army of Tennessee in 1862-63. Finally forced to remove him to avoid army mutiny, Davis stuns everybody by in effect promoting Bragg to the position of his Chief Military Advisor. From this perch, he schemes against his enemies, especially the large anti-Bragg faction in the Army of Tennessee. He also has a malicious key hand in the removal of Joe Johnston, who replaces him as army commander. Bragg pushes the removal and substitute of John Bell Hood. After Hood falls on his face, Bragg's influence wanes sharply. He is a most unlovable creature.

GENERAL KIRBY SMITH — D-

Another one of Jeff Davis' stranger picks for leadership. A junior commander in Virginia, he is sent to east Tennessee early on. In Bragg's attempted 1862 invasion of Kentucky, which might have actually worked, he refuses to co-operate. Davis then inexplicably promotes Smith to command the vast Confederate territory west of the Mississippi River called the TransMississippi Department. Smith promptly organizes what becomes known as Kirby Smithdom. He is good at logistics and organizes procurement of supplies from Europe through Mexico and his own-chartered blockade-rumers. He is also vigorous at encouraging home-grown war supportive industries or starting his own. In other words, he is a heck of a procurement clerk and empire builder.

Smith was vastly annoyed with Richard Taylor, his second in command who keeps wanting to fight and beat up on the Federals occupying part of the region. It is puzzling through the prism of time to fathom why Jeff Davis suffered a commander that ignored government directives, refused to coordinate holding the Mississippi River basin with comrades to the east and basically did his own thing, which was not much. Smith is a sort of Confederate McClellan. He's scared to use or damage the thing he helped create. The best you can say about the troops in Smith's department was that they were the best clothed, best fed, and best drilled in the entire Confederacy.

GENERAL ROBERT E. LEE — A

The best General for either side of the war and probably of all-American history. He had his best run in the eighteen months after Joe Johnston was severely wounded at the battle of Seven Pines in May 1862. Lee took over, built on his old friend's foundation, and formed the Army of Northern Virginia. He rang off a string of aggressive and dazzling victories with audacious tactics, but they came at a heavy price both in men and officers from his aggressive tactics. He formed a special bond to his men who called him "Marse Robert" with deep affection.

His army is the best the South has formed when almost everyone thought the war would be over within ninety days. When it turns into a long-protracted struggle, this army is chained to shielding capital Richmond not by choice but to avoid the loss of face by its fall.

Because of the nature of its formation, Lee's army had a large bulk of the pre-war Southern militia and the cream of the trained officers available. From those Lee weeded out the lacking to his standards and foisted them on the other regions of the South. So it is unfair to compare other Confederate forces to his army.

When he resigned from the Federal army at the war's outset, he publicly stated he took the action to defend his countrymen in his native state of Virginia. This was a common rhetoric by most resigning officers. Evidently Lee also meant it. That fateful day at Hull House the North lost its greatest soldier.

The war was not lost in the east but in the west. Nobody could get him to take command in the west when the war was being lost there. He declined the president several times and even the war cabinet, too, when asked to go west in 1863 to save Vicksburg and later Atlanta.

His health suffered severely in the war, and he likely had several heart attacks, including one in the summer of 1864. His high standard of duty and deference to authority caused him to soldier on.

He could only watch helplessly as Grant assaulted his weakened army in 1864 with unceasing frontal charges. Grant racked up 50,000 Federal losses in a mere six weeks. Still Lee and his men held Richmond albeit by being pinned into siege lines that stretch forty miles and robbed Lee of mobility.

He and his army came to be known as the epitome of Southern glory. Congress demanded Lee be made Commander in Chief and wished he would take over as a benevolent war dictator. Davis knew duty bound Lee would never skirt proper authority. Finally, when it is too late, Davis appointed Lee

Army Commander in Chief in 1865, knowing Lee would not buck him despite his personal desires.

By the end in 1865, Lee's Army of Northern Virginia is the only Rebel force that is hunted down and forced to surrender due to starvation. Why Lee did not remove more food reserves out of the warehouses and place it along the rail lines when he abandoned Richmond is a mystery given his careful nature of planning. More than likely, he was ordered to leave the food stuffs.

The ostensible plan was to slip away from Grant while the roads were still muddy from the winter and join Johnston to face Sherman traveling fast by rail. It is quite possible Lee never really wanted to leave Virginia. He becomes the first Confederate commander in 1865 to surrender a large force. As is to be expected, he gets the least generous terms.

He declines Grant's plea to overtly implore other Confederates to lay down their arms. Covertly he does exactly that.

Whether he ever altered his view of quick decisive battles to force the North to accommodation is unclear. If nothing else, his two big offensive failures at Antietam and Gettysburg failed to take into account the woeful limits of Confederate logistics, but he needed only to look at his barefoot, hungry men to realize this was the South's last chance to end the war with a victory.

GENERAL JOSEPH E. JOHNSTON — B+

"Old Joe" had one big failing. He could not get along with President Davis. He declined to placate Davis with smooth flattery as Lee did. And he would not give Davis the assurances he wanted to hold Atlanta at all costs, although he intended to do just that.

He gets great credit for rebuilding the morale and ability of the Army of Tennessee after Bragg's departure. He also did better stalling Sherman before Atlanta than Lee did with Grant before Richmond.

He was recalled after Hood almost wrecked the army, and Johnston stings Sherman twice as the blue armed mob pillages through the Carolinas in 1865. When Lee was unable to join Johnston and combine forces, there was no hope. The great mythical battle to hold off Sherman was untenable. His greatest achievement was that he worked out far more generous terms than Lee received and surrendered his men. In so doing, he ignored Davis' orders to disband and resort to guerilla warfare. His example serves as a template to other Southern commanders who followed his example.

GENERAL JOHN BELL HOOD — F

Hood really belonged to the 1861-62 era of the war when bumbling amateur armies were trying to mold green rookies into soldiers. Then you were a prized asset if you were brave, had a powerful voice, and could stand in front of nervous troops and yell "charge!" Unlike most other generals, Hood didn't learn and progress as the war grew far more sophisticated and deadly. He was a honcho brigade commander and a good division commander. That was the outer apex of his ability. His West Point roommate, Federal John Schofield, said not kindly that Hood was, well...just not a really bright candle. Hood loses an arm at Gettysburg and then a leg at Chickamauga. Wracked by pain, he comes to depend on Laudanum, a liquid distillation of opium.

Convalescing in Richmond in the winter of 1863-64, he ingratiated himself to President Davis, who forced him as a corps commander on the new Army of Tennessee commander Joe Johnston. Robert E. Lee and Pete Longstreet are Hood's old immediate superiors, know Hood's limits, and are aghast. While recovering Hood also clumsily entered Richmond society and made a spectacle of himself trying to court a wickedly precocious flirt named Sally Preston. Sally toys with him and leads him on for fun. He proposes, and she suggests she might consider if Hood were an army commander. Privately she tells her friends she never would marry a cripple or a dumb ox and that Hood is both. Love struck Hood believed her, and when he joins Johnston in Georgia, his actions lend overwhelming credence that he was plotting to topple Johnston and get the army command job. And you readers thought history is boring?

Hood blew several tactical actions, including a massive army size ambush Johnston has laid for the advancing Sherman. Even the trusting Johnston becomes suspicious. Parallel to this activity, Hood was secretly writing letters to Davis and Bragg in Richmond that are full of lies about Johnston's actions and what the gallant Hood would do. The poisonous deeds garner his wish, and Hood is promoted to supplant Johnston. The Sherman army rejoices, and the hapless Army of Tennessee is thrown in despair. The cripple is too immobile to be in command of anything, much less an army. Hood has an attack mandate, and he does so three major times in less than two weeks. He was soundly thumped, and the Army of Tennessee lost over 20,000 men, more than Johnston had lost in six months. He also lost Atlanta. Lincoln was re-elected, and Southern morale plummeted. If Hood had been decent, he would have resigned. Instead he blamed the setbacks on his men and calls them cowards, and this is by far the worst action any leader of men can take. While the rank and file may have despised Bragg and loved Johnston, they positively hated Hood.

Jeff Davis traveled down to look into matters. The army was drawn up for inspection. As Hood and Davis rode the ragged lines, the soldiers booed Hood, called him names, and sounded cheers of "bring back Old Joe!" Hood and Davis were deeply embarrassed. Davis predictably stood by his man. He appointed General Beauregard as theater commander to oversee Hood but granted him no authority. It is but a flimsy fig leaf of placation by Davis at his worst.

Hood tried to entice Sherman northward by raiding the railroad to Chattanooga and Sherman did follow him for a while. But soon Sherman wearied of bringing Hood to battle. Instead Sherman detached a big chunk of his army under "Rock of Chickamauga" Thomas and sent it north to Nashville. He then turned and began his infamous march to the sea.

In perhaps the strangest military dance of the war, two major armies marched away from each other to invade the other's territory while ignoring the defense of their own. Hood's fantastical plan was to take Nashville, push through Kentucky, and cross the Ohio River. He was supposed to get final approval from Beauregard. But by the time the Creole hears of Hood's march, he is long gone northward. Hood lacked the manpower, winter clothing, bridging equipment, and the logistical strength to even seriously threaten Nashville, and winter was looming dead ahead. In that era, armies didn't mount invasions of enemy territory in cold winter weather. His duty was to stop Sherman from ripping out the vital innards of the Confederacy and not to chase false glory. Hood tried to flank his old West Point roommate Schofield's force sent to slow him down while Thomas prepared to crush Hood.

But his retreating adversary steals a night march on a very drugged up Hood. Through that night, Hood's generals repeatedly wake him and ask him to do something, but he demurs.

In the morning, Hood is outraged and leashes out at his senior generals. He calls them all cowards and the men, too. Heated words are exchanged. Had Hood not been a cripple, it is very likely that the generals, including Cheatham and Forrest, would have run Hood through or shot him down.

Hood decided to punish his commanders by ordering a massive frontal attack on Schofield by the two-thirds of his army on the field. But his largest corps and all the artillery are not yet up. Forrest noted a battle is unnecessary and the Federals can be flanked upstream. The attack is far larger than the more famous Pickett's charge at Gettysburg, and over 6,000 Confederate veterans and seven generals were killed. The gloomy Rebels marched to battle with little hope and their names pinned on their backs with paper scraps. The wounded totals are staggering. Essentially the Army of Tennessee died that day.

There are two more major battles near Nashville, but Hood's army is wrecked. About six months later, 15,000 starving and tattered survivors of the 70,000 Johnston commanded limped into northern Mississippi at the end of 1864. Hood was unrepentant, blaming all his misfortunes on his officers and men. Finally he asked to be relieved, and Davis immediately granted the overdue wish. Hood was the only general on either side to effectively destroy a major army through his own massive incompetence and hatred of the entity he commanded.

GENERAL P.G.T. BEAUREGARD — C +

A vain New Orleanean Creole, he was pompous and a fantasy chaser. The "hero" of Fort Sumter should never have received the rank of full general and was probably best suited to commanding a division or a Charleston semi-backwater department. He performed capably after his failures at First Bull Run and Shiloh by defending the Carolina coast about Charleston. He lost favor with the administration with wild dreams of invasion using other general's troops and ignoring logistics.

His finest hour came when "Beast" Butler landed with over 45,000 Federals in May 1864 south of Richmond. Nominally in command of the area, he patched forces together to confront the invasion. His shrill cries for help went unheeded. He had exaggerated too much in the past. The stakes could not have been higher. Should Butler take Petersburg, the rail line's links spiking southward would be compromised. Then northbound supplies for Lee's ever hungry army would be cut off. Medical supplies and the vital "Nassau" bacon ran in by blockade runners to Wilmington, N.C. would be undeliverable. To his undying credit, Beauregard improvised and cobbled together a weird assortment of troops from his own department, transiting brigades shuttling around by rail in the Davis world of troop transfers and local militia. To command them, Beauregard relied on hapless George Pickett, who was under orders to return to Lee with his men. Lieutenant General D.H. Hill, the intellectually brilliant brother-in-law of Stonewall Jackson, served as a voluntary aide and de facto leader of this unwieldy mass. D.H. Hill's skill and Butler's incompetence resulted in a scratch force of 15,000 Rebels bottling up Butler's hosts in a rather useless peninsula called Bermuda Hundred.

Then Beauregard used his engineer's training to erect a strong series of fortifications about Petersburg that Lee will later occupy. Danger mollified he resorted to his old ways and tried to scheme for Lee's troops but not Lee. He fails of course. In the twilight months, he was supposed to oversee what Hood is doing. The crippled army leader wiggled away from him, exceeded his orders, and advanced into Tennessee. Thus Hood lost contact with Sherman's host in Georgia. So begins the largely uncontested "March to the Sea" of legend. Beauregard was furious at Hood but helpless to do anything. It was too late to get Hood's army back in front of Sherman.

Loyal to the end, Beauregard helped unselfishly where he could for the balance of the conflict. He was particularly effective gathering scattered units and remnants of others to Joe Johnston in the Carolinas in 1865.

LT. GENERAL RICHARD TAYLOR — A
Taylor was the highly able brother-in-law of President Davis through Davis' deceased first wife. He was the son of the late President Zackary Taylor, handsome, articulate, and extremely intelligent, a West Pointer and charismatic. He had it all. Winning plaudits for his abilities in Stonewall Jackson's great campaigns, he was transferred west to his native Louisiana.

It was hoped he would help bring some order to the Trans-Mississippi Dept. If anyone could have, he was the most likely man from the locale. Unfortunately Davis also sent Kirby Smith to run the department. Taylor watched helplessly as Smith frittered away chances to coordinate defense with Confederates along the Vicksburg-Port Hudson corridor in 1863. In spite of Smith, Taylor threatened and came close to retaking New Orleans. This was while the Federal forces of Banks were almost entirely upstream investing Port Hudson as Grant laid siege to Vicksburg.

Again, in 1864, Taylor, ignoring Smith's orders to retreat, concocted the great Confederate victories of the Federal Red River campaign at Mansfield and Pleasant Hill. He almost captured most of the Federal River fleet that would have reunited the two halves of the South. This would have certainly doomed Lincoln's chances for re-election. Instead the predictably battlefield inept Smith forced Taylor to send half his force at the veritable eve of success into the road poor boondocks of Arkansas to foil a Federal force attempting to produce just that result. Taylor wrote his brother-in-law that he would no longer serve under scoundrel Smith and demanded a transfer.

Normally that would have resulted in Davis blacklisting an uppity general and consigning him to the involuntarily retired scrap heap. Davis transferred Taylor to command Stephen D. Lee's Department of Mississippi, Alabama and east Louisiana while Lee was sent to corps command in the Army of Tennessee to replace the just promoted Hood. A much more lucid selection based on sheer results and talent would have been to leave Lee where he ably was and send Taylor to corps command instead. Taylor was a major wasted talent, a difference maker forced to make none.

LT. GENERAL NATHAN BEDFORD FORREST — A

What superlative can you use? The "Wizard of the Saddle" was the most unused talent of the Confederacy. Lee and Davis so opined after the war. Part of the reason Grant, Sherman, and other field commanders granted such generous capitulation terms in 1865 was the fear that Forrest would lead a massive guerilla campaign at war's end using paroled veterans. He doesn't, of course. Indeed he gave his men a written farewell address that surpassed Lee's in eloquence and was a forward look to restoration of peaceful authority.

He had no peer in tactical skill in the use of mounted infantry. And he was an excellent judge of character. He was disgusted with Bragg squandering the victory of Chickamauga. It is telling that he implied fatal physical harm to Bragg in late 1863 if he crossed his path again. He was enraged the crippled Hood called his army and generals and troops cowards just before the awful battle of Franklin in late 1864. Only Hood's disability dissuaded Forrest from running him through with his sword. Since Forrest personally killed at least twenty-eight men in close combat in the war, his words were not idle threats. In dispassionate theoretical terms one can't help but wonder about what might have been had Forrest dispatched either of those worthies.

MAJOR GENERAL PATRICK CLEBURNE — A

Even Jeff Davis labeled him the "Stonewall of the West." The Arkansan was the best division commander of probably what was the best division in the South. His division flew a distinctive blue St. Andrew's cross flag. The very sight of it caused trepidation to Federals opposite their lines. He was a major under-utilized talent. He was long overdue for corps command.

In early 1864, he made the "mistake" of suggesting in a confidential circular to the generals and colonels of the Army of Tennessee that any slaves that wanted to fight for the Confederacy should be granted freedom. His idea was not new, and everybody knew that plenty of free blacks and servant blacks were already fighting for the South. Indeed it was common knowledge that any black captured in Confederate uniform was summarily shot when reaching prison camps, if not before. But the idea was too premature for Jeff Davis. Instead Davis ordered the circular suppressed and Cleburne blacklisted from future promotion.

At the terrible slaughter at Franklin, Tennessee in late 1864, General Cleburne was killed, along with six other Confederate generals leading their men from the front with sword in one hand and a pistol in the other. Nearby his best friend, Texan Hiram Granbury, is also killed almost simultaneously leading his brigade. Perhaps the most telling memory of the two generals is when the Texan survivors go home after the war and name two sister towns southwest of Fort Worth...Cleburne and Granbury.

MAJOR GENERAL DABNEY MAURY — B+

A solid leader and organizer, he was perhaps the perfect man to defend Mobile Bay, Mobile and the southern portion of the Tombigbee Valley. And he did so with fairly limited manpower and often had his garrison depleted by levies for other flash points, particularly Atlanta and northern Mississippi. Virtually overlooked then and now, he defended the last major unscathed Confederate area east of the Mississippi River with concentrated agricultural production, military armaments manufacture, and ample road, rail, and water transportation. Federal Admiral Farragut took the outer forts of Mobile Bay in latter 1864.

It was but a toehold. The bay and the entire region above remained unfettered Confederate territory. In April 1865, when Lee's army was enduring its literal death march to Appomattox, a massive Federal land invasion occurred. As Lee's army was surrendering, Maury's defiant force of some 15,000 fought the last major battles of the war. Casualties were heavy with over 1,000 dead. Maury's force included a big chunk of the remnant survivors of the Army of Tennessee. Consequently, in the last great struggle, all thirteen Confederate states had at least one distinct organized unit, plus Maryland and the Indian Territory (Oklahoma). In good order, Maury abandoned Mobile while preparing to defend the Valley. Weeks later, when solid word that Johnston had folded reaches Maury, he surrendered on the same general terms. His decision had much influence on the surrender of Nathan Bedford Forrest.

MAJOR GENERAL JOSEPH WHEELER — D-

He was something of a "wannabe," J.E.B. Stuart. Despite the plumed hat, he couldn't pull it off. He had neither the intelligence nor the discipline to tame and mold his rather wild cavalry. In 1864 he chafed and agitated at the tight leash Joe Johnston imposed on him. Grudgingly he used his men as dismounted infantry, and they performed well in that role.

When Hood succeeded Johnston, he sent Wheeler to smash Sherman's line of communications and vital rail line artery. He made a halfhearted ineffectual effort to tear up some rails. Then his men ignored his orders and galloped off all the way to the trackless wastes of east Tennessee. He should have been fired. The absence of his cavalry resulted in Hood's lines being too short in length. This was to be a major catalyst in the loss of Atlanta.

LT. GENERAL STEPHEN LEE — C+

This handsome, honorable man was probably thrust into more prominence than he sought or was capable of at a fairly young age. He was no relation to the aristocratic Lee family of Virginia. But early in the war, under Stonewall Jackson, he distinguishes himself as an artillery commander. He was sent to Vicksburg and helped direct the erection of the defense there and placement of the guns. Assigned a division of infantry, he is surrendered and paroled with the rest of the garrison.

In late 1863, he assumed command of the Department of Mississippi, Alabama, and east Louisiana. His two principal subordinates are the capable Dabney Maury commanding around Mobile and the legendary Nathan Bedford Forrest in northern Mississippi. His only blunder was in ordering Forrest to make a frontal assault at Harrisburg, Mississippi the summer of 1864. He wanted to rush Maury's borrowed troops back to Mobile to greet what turns out to be a false invasion alarm.

He was abruptly selected for corps command in the Army of Tennessee to plug the gap created by the departure of Johnston and the ascension of Hood. He is aggressively rash in the last of the three major attacks Hood launched after assuming command. It cost his corps severely. But he learned from experience and perhaps reflects on the mechanics of what Stonewall Jackson did. He served with ever improving skill and led his corps to the end in North Carolina in 1865.

In his twilight, as the senior surviving Confederate general, he writes and delivers the "charge" or heritage directions to the sons and descendants of the war veterans as they organize the Sons of Confederate Veterans. This heritage organization of about 50,000 remains to this day.

BRIG. GENERAL ISAAC ST. JOHN — A

St. John was everything Northrop was not. Robert E. Lee, when appointed Commander in Chief of all Confederate forces in February 1865, quickly moved to fire the despised Northrop. In conjunction with also new Secretary of War Breckinridge, St. John was selected as the replacement. Previously he had been the organizing miracle master behind the Niters bureau that provided the raw materials to Gorgas's Ordnance Bureau. In less than three months, he had drastically improved the food supply from the shrunken territory that Lee and Johnston's forces occupied. One can only wonder about the failure to apply his talents far sooner to the perennially chronic food situation for Confederates east of the Mississippi River.

LT. GENERAL JAMES "PETE" LONGSTREET — A

Joe Johnston was the army level proponent of the defensive attrition warfare to wear down Northern resolve. This concept included occasional counter punches in order to conserve irreplaceable veterans. Longstreet was the corps level equivalent to that creed. In late 1863, he was sent with his corps from Virginia to northern Georgia to help Braxton Bragg. His skill almost won the battle of Chickamauga. He secured a massive defeat of the Federal forces but had to settle for no more. Bragg's dawdling ineptitude in following up on the victory caused mutual tensions leading to the near mutiny of the senior officers. Jeff Davis himself has to come to settle matters. The president is blind to reality, and Bragg retained command for a while.

Longstreet is sent on a useless expedition to recapture Knoxville but mainly to get him away from Bragg. Knoxville was one giant fortress and not worth the cost. Longstreet marched his corps all the way back to Virginia over the mountains to rejoin Lee. The second day of the battle of Wilderness in May 1864, Longstreet devised and led a strong improvised counter punch to an early dawn assault led by Union General Hancock and his Second Corps. Longstreet was badly wounded by his own men in broad daylight in the wilderness thickets just a few miles from where Stonewall Jackson met the same fate.

Longstreet survived and came back early with a writing arm unusable for that purpose. He learned to write with the other and is a welcome unexpected return to Lee's circle of confidants. From then, until the surrender at Appomattox, he was reassuring, calm, and an analytical force behind Lee's decisions. His theories on the futility of frontal charges against even hasty breastworks in an era of modern firepower were way ahead of their time.

Many tens of thousands of soldiers paid the ultimate price both in the Civil War and later in World War I as a sad result of their commanders lacking "Old Pete's" perception. He was a very solid tactician and the best all-around corps commander the Confederacy had in the war. He may not have been as shining on the offensive as fellow corps leader Stonewall Jackson, but the war of 1864 to 1865 was not that of 1862 to 1863.

LT. GENERAL A.P. HILL — A

When Stonewall Jackson was wounded and died of pneumonia in early 1863, Lee reorganized his infantry into three corps. Trusty Longstreet retained one, and the others went to Dick Ewell and A.P. Hill. Formerly Hill commanded the largest and many said best division in the army. It was called the "Light Division," a misnomer if there ever was one. Hill is not brilliant at Gettysburg, but nobody was.

In the fall of 1863, in the short-lived Mine Run campaign, he got part of his men snared in a large ambush and needlessly lost a couple thousand men. He grieved, for he is perhaps the most "modern" of the Confederate generals. A West Pointer, but not of the aristocracy like so many of Lee's generals, he loved and was beloved by the common soldier.

He found his old stride in the Battle of the Wilderness and never lost it thereafter. He also learned from his experiences and became a quiet rock on which Lee could depend in the dark season of the trenches in the last half of 1864 and through early 1865. His Ill Corps becomes Lee's last mobile stroking arm, and Hill repeatedly used it with great skill defending Lee's right flank, turning back the enemy, and inflicting great loss on Federal advances. He even wrecked the vaunted Federal Il Corps forever. In that terribly cold winter of starvation in 1864-65, "Little Powell," as his men affectionately called him, made daily rounds of the ghastly trenches, giving encouragement and seeing to his men. While the frequently ill Hill was doing his duty, many fellow generals took leaves of absence, reported themselves sick, or lived in appropriated large houses.

The end came as Lee commenced his abandonment of the Richmond-Petersburg line. It was Hill's corps that bore the brunt of Grant's massive assault. Most of the men were killed or captured fighting to the final trenches.

Hill fell dead with pistol in hand demanding the surrender of two Federal privates that had broken through. He had publicly stated for months he did not wish to survive the fall of his hometown Petersburg.

A visibly shaken Lee says of the news, "He is at peace now and it is we who remain that must suffer." There is absolutely no substitute for a good man.

LT. GENERAL RICHARD "DICK" EWELL — F

A brilliant division commander under Stonewall Jackson, his loss of a leg took more away from him than part of a limb. Outwardly he displayed the same old pleasant, if somewhat eccentric ways. Inwardly he had lost his ability to be analytical and make decisions. First displayed at Gettysburg in 1863, this trait continued into 1864 at the Wilderness and Spotsylvania. Six weeks into that campaign, Lee had to fire him. He was officially relieved for "illness."

Finally he was assigned to the rag tag home guard militia of Richmond. He led his old men, young boys, and government clerks south as Lee abandoned Richmond in April 1865. Ewell managed to botch a turn in the road, and perhaps a fourth of Lee's shrinking band was captured at Saylor's Creek after a nasty hand-to-hand fight. Ewell is one of several generals captured. To his captors, he bitterly denounced Lee for continuing a "hopeless" struggle for the past year.

Publicly castigating icon Lee and the enemy to boot, this is a major no-no. Later word of the episode reaches Lee's veterans and his old comrades-in-arms largely shunned Ewell after the war.

MAJOR GENERAL JUBAL EARLY — C

A grizzled, profane, and dour man, Lee respected him greatly and fondly called him "my mean old man." Actually Lee was the older of the two! Selected by Lee to replace the bumbling Richard Ewell as his Il Corps commander, he performed capably. Lee, besieged about Richmond by summer 1864, trusted him enough to detach a fair part of his mobile force to imitate Stonewall Jackson's 1862 expeditions towards Washington via the Shenandoah Valley. Early got to the outer ramparts of Washington. And his sharp shooters even took pot shots at Lincoln, who came out to have a look at real war. But it is 1864. Grant detached great force under Sheridan, and Early must retreat.

After a series of time consuming seesaw battles, ruthless Sheridan finally crushed Early and destroyed the great Valley as a source of food and provender for Lee's starving army. In spite of the hopeless odds, the public and the politicians howled for Early's head as the fall guy. Lee has no choice but to send Early home in false disgrace. Early deserved a better fate, sour personality or not.

MAJOR GENERAL JOHN B. GORDON — B+

The non-professional soldier leaped from brigade to division to Il corps command in less than a year. That would have been a stratospheric climb, even for a West Pointer. He was gallant, smart, audacious, and charismatic. His last-ditch plan to assault the Union center in April 1865 was approved by a desperate Lee looking for a diversion, so his army could flee its trenches and try to join forces with Joe Johnston in North Carolina. It was a forlorn chance and cost Lee 6,000 irreplaceable Il Corps veterans.

Gordon's finest moment came a week later leading the formal surrender of troops at Appomattox to a saluting Federal General Chamberlain and his equally respectful troops. Gordon and men returned the gesture and set the tone of how the veterans on both sides felt about each other and themselves. Twelve years of bitter and oppressive "reconstruction" lay ahead, but the veterans on both sides retained their grudging respect and admiration for each other.

MAJOR GENERAL J.E.B. STUART — A

The flamboyant cavalryman's adolescent raiding around in the great Gettysburg campaign of 1863 cost the South dearly. But he learned his lesson. By 1864 General Stuart was a different, more somber man. In the spring of 1864, he was glued to the approaching host of Grant/Meade and served perfectly as the eyes of Lee's army with the Wilderness loss of severely wounded.

RATING THE GENERALS OF THE NORTH
1864-1865

MAJOR GENERAL WILLIAM T. SHERMAN — A

Sherman had the ability to accept orders from Grant without question and execute them post haste. That alone distinguished him along with his understanding of the everyday soldier under his command. He did not waste his men in battle and provided well for them, and they respected him for it. His march to the sea and his subsequent march north to Tennessee was a testament to his men's physical and mental toughness, and that state of mind came from their commander.

LIEUTENANT GENERAL U.S. GRANT — A

Grant is the first Lieutenant General since George Washington and in command of the Army of the Potomac, and finally, all Union Forces. He has an understanding of his numeric superiority and uses it to the fullest. He is better armed, supplied, and loaded with manpower and uses it to the fullest extent possible in battles.

MAJOR GENERAL GEORGE BRINTON MCCLELLAN — B-

McClellan was not even a good tactical commander, but he brought to the Army of the Potomac, in its worst hour, what it needed the most - training!

All great military leaders have an understanding that training builds confidence among everyday soldiers, and he did that. He gave them a workable chain of command that would serve them in years to come.

MAJOR GENERAL PHILIP SHERIDAN — A

Little Phil was a fine commander and as good a Calvary commander present in the Civil War. President Lincoln, when asked what the ideal Calvary officer would look like, said "about six-foot tall." He later told Sheridan that he revised his statement and 5' 2" was just fine, and of course, that was the height of Phil Sheridan.

MAJOR GENERAL GEORGE ARMSTRONG CUSTER — B

Custer was loved, hated, disliked, dashing, courageous, and stupid, but he gave his due in the Civil War. He did a great deal to help the North win the war as an outstanding Calvary Officer. His motto was "Ride to the sounds of the guns," and he did that well. While in the Army, I had an occasion to serve at Fort George Armstrong Custer in Michigan. The place was in shambles, and I had tears in my eyes. That emotion turned to my ripping into an officer in charge of the facility!

MAJOR GENERAL GEORGE MEADE — C

Meade had a defining moment in his military service at the Gettysburg battle. Even though the casualties were about even, the South's ability to wage war on Northern ground was over. Meade failed to pursue Lee's army, and if he had, the war would have been over and countless lives spared. Lee in his dispatches said he was shocked that Meade didn't follow up with a massive action to end the war. Lee could not believe his good fortune and retreated to fight another day. President Lincoln was enraged at Meade for letting this chance to end the war slip by him.

MAJOR GENERAL JOHN BUFORD — B+

Buford arrived at Gettysburg with his Calvary and secured the high ground, which was the ideal location to engage Lee's forces. He came in from the south, but as the day one battle took place, he wisely dispatched a rider to request that John Reynolds bring his large force up immediately to help secure the high ground, including Big and Little Roundtop for excellent artillery positioning.

MAJOR GENERAL JOSHUA LAWRENCE CHAMBERLIN — A

Chamberlin may have done more than anyone to bring all fighting to an end and promote A Miracle of War. Following Lee's surrender, the balance of CSA forces under General Gordon, which may have been in excess of 18,000 soldiers, came to surrender to Chamberlin. He orders no cheering, no remarks to be made, and their best blue uniforms with yellow capes to be worn. Upon Gordon's arrival, the Union troops lined each side of the road and gave a crisp salute. Some were crying. It was a show of respect from soldier to soldier. Chamberlin's military tactics can be found in our Gettysburg Chapter.

9 798888 729 1475